Stefanie Dawn

The Demon in Me
An Unearthly Sins Novel

Stefanie Dawn

This book is a work of fiction. Any references to real events, real people, and real places are used fictitiously. Other names, characters, places and incidents are products of the Author's imagination and any resemblance to persons, living or dead, actual events, organisations or places is entirely coincidental.

All rights are reserved. This book is intended for the purchaser of this book ONLY. No part of this book may be reproduced or transmitted in any form or by any means, graphic, electronic, or mechanical, including photocopying, recording, taping, or by any information storage retrieval system, without the express written permission of the Author. All songs, song titles and lyrics contained in this book are the property of the respective songwriters and copyright holders.

Disclaimer: The material in this book contains graphic language and sexual content and is intended for mature audiences, ages 18 and older.

ISBN: 978-1763870413

Editing and Proofing by Swish Design & Editing
Book Design by Swish Design & Editing
Cover design by Opium House Creatives
Published by Angels and Fire Books
Cover Image Copyright 2021

DEDICATION

To the tall, dark, and handsome man in my life.
The strong and silent type who offers his
unwavering support for my writing journey.

To the dark men who live only within my
imagination.
May they all come out to play in my books.

the
DEMON
in me
AN UNEARTHLY SINS NOVEL

PROLOGUE

What do you do when you leave hell and plan on living it up on Earth?

Not simply for a visit like the others.

Not those little holidays demons took. A break from hell to wreak havoc on those humans still living, a change of scenery from tortured souls.

But leaving hell to live on Earth, permanently.

No going back.

So, what's the plan?

Blend in—that one is obvious.

Become qualified—so there won't be as much suspicion when you rise through the ranks.

While you could've done it on influence alone and gained any position you wanted, any home, or any human to be by your side, relying entirely on your supernatural influence seemed somewhat redundant when trying to rid yourself of the place. No. It was done with education, experience, and just enough charm to work your way up, and then when you're CEO of one of the largest architecture firms in the state, with your sights set on nationwide expansion, you no longer *needed* to use your powers.

At least, not all the time.

You've worked yourself up to a position where money is not a concern. You have acquired a penthouse apartment, and then you're the absolute fucking poster child of a rich bachelor. Your behavior from here on out is expected—partying, womanizing, and nothing you do surprises people because they expect this shit from anyone in your position.

It's so overt, it's covert.

So, what's next, you ask?

Now you're here, what else are you on Earth for?

Fun, fights, feasts, and, of course, plenty of God's greatest gift—fucking.

CHAPTER
1

Charlotte

He was yelling at me again.

What had I done this time?

From what I could tell, it was the audacity to have friends that weren't him. He said they were all trying to turn me against him, and he wasn't the problem, they were. As he continued to yell, I looked anywhere but at his face, scanning the floor and ceiling, letting my eyes flit around the room. It was a strain to resist the urge to stretch my neck as I looked around, lest he realized I was refusing to make eye contact. That would only be another sign he'd take as an open invitation to scream at me for not listening.

I was listening, I just didn't care anymore.

I didn't want to look at him.

I simply couldn't take one more day of

watching the red flush creep up from his neck, the way his ears changed color before his cheeks did, the way he bit his lip in between bouts of yelling as though he was holding something back.

If this was what he let go, I hated to think what he was holding back.

Looking at the walls didn't help. They were adorned with photos of us together, smiling through the lies—windows to a world that didn't exist beyond the outward appearance on social media. Lies that disappeared the moment the flash from the camera died away.

But this time, I was done with him. I'd be leaving, and I wouldn't let him follow me because now, I had a reason he couldn't refuse. No doubt, he'd try to blame me, but I had a solid excuse to walk away.

For I had seen him with her.

He hadn't exactly been hiding it well. The way he left the room whenever his cell phone chimed. The smell of the other woman's perfume on his skin as he moved on top of me for three minutes of pumping before he was done, and ultimately, I was left unsatisfied.

Sex was better with my ex, I'm sure of it. But it had been so long since I had been with someone else, maybe it was only better in my head.

It was definitely better in my head.

They had been together at a club, their tongues

grotesquely fighting for dominance coupled with obscene sounds of pleasure just in case anyone unfortunate enough to be near them was under any illusions about what was happening. The images swam before my eyes, and then those images were moving across the walls behind him as he continued to yell, projected by my mind, I'm sure. But it was so clear, a movie reel reminding me why I was doing this.

As if I needed another reason.

But I wasn't upset or angry.

Only relieved.

Because I was right, *I had been right all along, and he couldn't say anything that would make me stay. Really, I should've listened to my gut instincts long ago—long before he pretty much cut all my friends from my life and long before he cut me off from myself and my goals. There was* nothing *he could say now to convince me it was my fault.*

Turning while he continued to yell at my retreating back, I held my head high before slamming the front door behind me. The fresh air felt amazing compared to the smell of sweat and shoes that seemed to always linger in his apartment. His voice was extinguished the moment the door had closed, and I was alone in the welcomed silence.

Silence.

The blanket of night swept across the suburb. I

didn't remember the sun setting. How late was it?

I walked.

Something felt wrong as I made my way down the street. Shouldn't I have bags? My shoulders felt light, too light. I wasn't carrying anything. Then I became aware I had no handbag, no phone, no keys—nothing I'd usually consider essential.

It didn't matter, I was leaving him, and it was the right thing to do. Jutting my chin out again, I strode down the empty road.

As the chill from the night air seeped through my useless shirt and caressed my skin, I hugged my arms around myself. I had no jacket. Another thing I'd usually have—the ever-practical Charlotte. The chill left a trail of goosebumps on my skin in its wake.

The streetlights came on as I walked, creating cones of light along the otherwise darkened asphalt. Looking up, I watched as they flickered on and off, throwing my face into a pantomime of shadow and light. Something still felt wrong, a feeling that was creeping up my spine and making me shudder. Looking back, I didn't recognize any of the houses, and the street stretched out infinitely behind me.

Where was I going?

Where was I now?

There was a presence near me. I couldn't see any movement, but I knew someone was there.

Everything beyond my shadow was darkness— not even an outline of a stranger intruded on my line of sight as I walked in and out of the unreliable light. The awareness was just there, the knowledge that someone was watching me. I never considered myself to be particularly in tune with my instincts, but now, I simply knew it to be true.

The feeling had started slowly. It bubbled beneath my skin with discomfort that grew until it felt as though there were eyes everywhere. I still couldn't see them, and that only made it worse— just me, the darkness, and the knowledge that I was being watched. The feeling came from every tree, every house corner, and every pothole in the uneven road, every one of them stabbing into my back.

The street became a tunnel of darkness as all the streetlights near me went out at once.

I stood in a haze of black, the nearest light too far to help see through the fog.

The fog? That wasn't there a moment before.

The distant light supplied only an eerie glow and did nothing to decrease my feeling of unease.

Where did the fog come from?

As I turned on the spot, I searched for anything familiar.

God, all I needed now was a horror movie soundtrack, and this night would be complete.

Walking faster than before, I pulled on my thin shirt as if the closeness of the impractical fabric could protect me from the cold. The trees creaked as they swayed. Ignoring them, I kept walking. But I made the mistake of looking back, and every branch and vine reached toward me while shadowy fingers beckoned me into the dark with them.

It's a trick of the light, right?

Then they reached for me. Actually. Reached.

The trees leaned in over the road from the pathway, creating an impenetrable archway as the first vine crawled around my ankle, twisting itself into a knotted mess and snagging my skin. Screaming, I was yanked from my feet, the crunch of my back against the road the only sound aside from my voice.

The air shifted, and the vine dragged me. Achingly slowly, pulling me from the misleading safety of the street toward the woods, every crevice in the road snagged at my hair and tore my clothes as if I needed another way to feel vulnerable. Swiping around in vain, I grabbed at everything, anything that might be my savior from the darkness. But there was nothing around to latch on to, only the fog I couldn't see through and the vine that pulled me into the all-encompassing darkness.

My head knocked on the curb as I was dragged

over it, then there were more vines. They came out of the fog and wrapped themselves around my wrists and elbows. They tugged at my knees and ankles, winding up my calves and pulling until my legs were held open in an invitation that made me choke back the bile rising in my throat.

Then I saw those eyes through the darkness. Those yellow eyes flashed with promise as he approached, tapping his slender fingers against his chest.

Those eyes.

The eyes that had haunted my childhood, that were in every dark room, every alleyway, and hid around every corner.

I opened my mouth to scream.

Sitting bolt upright in bed, my tank top was damp with sweat. Stretching my fingers out, I tried to ease the ache in them from the way I had been gripping and tearing at the sheets. Remembering where I was, I clasped my hands over my mouth, listening for any indication that I had woken my roommate with the scream that had escaped my lips. When there was nothing, I took some deep, steadying breaths, trying unsuccessfully to calm myself. Reaching for the glass of water on the bedside table, I fumbled and knocked it to the floor.

Mumbling, "Shit," I pulled my bathrobe off the foot of the bed and threw it over the spill. I'd deal with that tomorrow.

My heart was still pounding in my chest. Holding a hand to my breast, goosebumps sprang up under my touch as I closed my eyes, trying to control my heart rate through will alone. Before any of this, before the nightmares, I had thought that the saying was figurative, *heart pounding in your chest.* It sounded painful and unrealistic.

But I felt it now, the almost literal feeling of my heart hammering against the back of my rib cage in a frenzied attempt to pull me from the danger in my mind. I wondered if my roommate, Meredith, would think less of me if I started sleeping with a night light like a child. Meredith would want to know why. Not out of some sick curiosity to use against me later but from a genuine concern that sprung only from true friendship. She was the sort of woman who cared deeply for others while keeping an air of aloofness about her that fooled no one.

Meredith was too nice for her own good, and I didn't want to have her rethink her offer for me to live with her temporarily because I was waking up at all hours screaming with night terrors.

Rubbing my eyes, I was forced to relive the images in my mind, burned into the back of my retinas. Although they were slightly different, now they were tied in with memories from my recent past.

It seemed the nightmares from my youth were back.

Frank

Slowly, I awoke.

Painfully regaining my sense of self as the sunlight assaulted my eyelids, I kept them closed in an attempt to hide from the dawning day. When I rolled over in the luxurious bed, I was impeded by a body. Groaning loudly, I tried the other side, my lip curling into a snarl when I was met with another block.

Growling deep in my throat, I swallowed back the urge that clawed up within me to fight my way free and thrash about at whatever was blocking me from my goal.

Which was, in this case, coffee.

As I sat up, I rubbed my hands vigorously across my face and over the three days of stubble, serving as a reminder that I hadn't been to the office as often as I should have. Opening my eyes, I smirked as my gaze wandered over the four naked women scattered across the mattress, laying at odd angles, having fallen asleep, or passed out, wherever they lay from the previous night.

Oh yes. I remembered.

Grinning, my teeth were slightly sharper than an

average human—something I had decided I liked and wasn't going to get cosmetically fixed—as the images from the previous night came back to me in flashes of flesh and alcohol.

Despite the demon blood that ran through my veins, alcohol and drugs on Earth had an interesting effect on me, revving me up instead of slowing me down. There was no crash, just a slow burn of excess energy that lasted for hours. The only downside, I somewhat lost control over my supernatural strength and had to be extra cautious not to cause unwelcome harm.

Unless I wanted to cause harm, then free play.

Relishing in the memories of the previous night—the echoes of the women's moans against my hot skin as I thrust into them rang in my ears. One after the other while the remaining women kept themselves entertained in front of me— touching, licking, and grinding against each other. These were memories I'd lock away for another night because now that's all they were—memories.

As day broke, I found my need for human company had evaporated.

"Out," I said, raising my voice enough to wake the women.

They stirred but didn't move.

"Get. Out."

If the volume wasn't enough to make them move, the tone certainly was. The women sat up and bounded off the bed after glancing at my face, my impatience caused my features to twist into something else, something darker. The mattress shifted under their weight as they each went their own way, gathering their clothes and dressing as they headed toward the door of the penthouse apartment. At least two of them glanced back, perhaps hoping for a sign they were welcome to stay or return for another round following the night before. But I ignored them, lying back with my hands linked behind my head until they left.

Sighing loudly when the front door closed, I was left alone with the silence and the lingering scent of sex. I stretched out, making a spectacle with a loud growl before reluctantly rolling until I was at the edge of the mattress, groaning dramatically with each turn before eventually sitting and sliding off the bed and walking naked to prepare a coffee.

Yeah, drugs and alcohol had an interesting effect, but caffeine still helped bring me back in line. Besides, I was fond of the routine—a morning coffee, a drink in the evening, maybe a wine with lunch some days. Part of the thrill lay in keeping a mundane routine when, behind the scenes, I still had to partake in other activities to keep my demon controlled. Every other night I'd have company, but I didn't want to get soft on humans too much, so having them stay the night was unusual. Company to provide pleasures of the flesh and remind me exactly why I was here and how much better it felt to be free.

Glancing at the calendar on the refrigerator, I sipped my coffee—*that coffee machine was an excellent investment.* Tomorrow I'd be running interviews for my new personal assistant. I had no problems with the last one, who was knowledgeable and had no issue with my dirty sense of humor. But after almost a decade in the industry, most recently as my assistant, she had now retired. It was well deserved, and I had spoiled her during her final week with flowers, jewelry, and chocolates, all those things that make human women drop their underwear. Or, in Abigail's case, roll her eyes and laugh as I'd wink at her while she thought me young enough to be her son.

The truth is, I may have tortured her great-grand-relatives in hell.

As an added bonus to hiring a new employee, anyone who didn't make the cut for my assistant might make it to my bedroom. In the past, I found sleeping with employees caused more problems than it was worth. The women I encountered tended to be either clingy or expect something more beyond the night of pleasure I offered. Honestly, I'd have thought multiple orgasms was enough to satiate them to move on after I got bored, but apparently, they wanted companionship. After all this time, I still didn't understand why humans wouldn't give themselves into physical pleasure and leave it as that. I couldn't help but smirk—all they needed was a night with me.

Sounds arrogant, right? Hard not to be when it's true.

Occasionally, demons bonded, but that seemed awfully limiting in a world full of possibilities.

Women of Earth would learn the benefits of separating physical pleasure from emotional connections, even if I had to teach them one at a time.

I found myself watching a movie reel of recent conquests in my mind. The potential for new meat made me think of all the delicious sounds they made the first time I took their panties down and pressed my tongue to the warmth underneath, already wet before I even laid a finger on them or in them. Shaking my head, I snapped myself out of the stupor when I realized I was palming my erection, practically rutting against the kitchen island. It looks like the women last night didn't wear me out as much as I did them. Human women were great, but demon females could fuck for days.

It seems I needed to take part in the other outlet I used to control the demon in me.

CHAPTER
2

Charlotte

You look fat in that. The voice in my head was loud, so I had to be louder.

"I like this one," I called over the door in the fitting room cubicle.

"Let me see," Meredith said.

Stepping out of the room, I wiggled my toes against the worn carpet as Meredith took in the tight dress. The black faded into an elegant gray as it moved up my body to a high neck. Something about the ombre look made me feel sophisticated. Perhaps it was the change of posture I needed to don to get the full effect of the dress's cut.

"Needs more boobs."

"Meredith," I chastised, but any seriousness to my tone was undermined by the grin on my face.

She shrugged. "They're your best asset."

"What? Not my ass?" Turning, I shook my hips, offbeat and exaggerated movements that left Meredith laughing, and my face flushed with embarrassment when the salesgirl looked at me with a raised brow and no hint of humor. Scurrying back into the fitting room, I hurried to try on the next dress.

This outfit was worse. Huffing, I cast a glanced over my shoulder at the door. It was a mistake to let Meredith take control of the choice of dresses. This was a job interview for an office, not a strip club. As I looked down at my cleavage, a small smile played across my lips. Well, Meredith was right about something—they were a decent asset. Distracted, I let my hands run over my breasts, pausing to tease my nipples with my fingers. Glancing over my shoulder again, I eyed the flimsy lock on the door.

How quickly could I get myself off?

Pausing, I let my arms drop to my sides and squeezed my eyes shut in a moment of self-chastising. What the hell was wrong with me? Getting off in a fitting room? No *way* was this something that would've crossed my mind even six months ago.

I never considered myself a particularly sexual person, but once I was away from Joshua and in a new city, it was like a switch had been flicked inside me. It was like I'd broken free of binds that had held me, and this city had somehow invigorated me, and a sexual awakening was apparently how my mind and body were expressing themselves now.

I'd only had one partner since coming here—a one-night stand after a night out with Meredith and some of her friends—and after a few drinks, I simply decided that since I had no plans to see him again, I could let myself go. Complete freedom in the bedroom, so I had made all the sounds that came naturally and completely disregarded whatever *image* that portrayed. He'd responded with equal enthusiasm, and it had been one of the best orgasms of my life.

So far, anyway.

However, after our romp, he had promptly fallen asleep. While I was still ready for round two, once again leaving me ultimately unsatisfied, except now I was alone with this part of myself newly awoken.

My fingers twitched as I reveled in the idea of finding something better.

Moving had been the best decision despite how difficult it had been and the emotional toll it had taken. Not only had it closed the door on a past with so many elements I'd rather forget, but it had also opened my life to new possibilities and experiences, both of which I planned to take every advantage of.

However, I needed two things—a steady job and money—and the confidence to leave Joshua in my past where he belonged and keep him out of my head where he seemed to have taken residence.

When alone with my thoughts or Meredith, I'd admit that the move terrified me. I had changed *everything* about my life in one fell swoop, so who wouldn't be afraid? But what was it they said? *Fake it until you make it*, and I could plaster on a confident facade as well as the best of them.

Changing back into my clothes—jeans that were slightly too tight, but I couldn't bring myself to get rid of because of how good they made my legs look, and a sleeveless button-up shirt—I snatched the dress of choice off the hanger and inspected it, my face dropping when I looked at the tag. It was more than I'd usually spend, and with my savings dwindling, I probably shouldn't, but this wasn't just any interview, and I wanted to have that extra *wow* factor. This was the big one, the chance I had been hoping for since moving, and before, although I never told anyone. So, while my hope mingled with all the doubt that it may not happen, I kept my mouth shut, lest I make it a reality by voicing my fear.

I couldn't get ahead of myself. I didn't have the job yet, but even scoring an interview was a feat worth celebrating.

Showing Meredith my dress of choice, she nodded her approval.

Looking at it again, I sighed. "Joshua would hate it."

My tone was without glee, as I took no pleasure in doing something he'd despise. The man had gotten inside my head in the worst way, eating away at my confidence until he had all the power, and I had nothing. Consequently, I still judged myself by his standards, and despite making the move, I had found it hard to shake his voice from my mind. He silently reminded me that I wasn't good enough and never would be.

I was sick of it.

I wanted that control back.

At night when I couldn't sleep, when all I could hear was the memories of him bellowing through the bedroom door, I'd imagine the life I was going to build for myself. I'd force the images of my past out of my mind and replaced them with my dreams for the future. Sure, it may be a naïve thing to do, but having the goal kept me focused, and it had been the only thing that had given me the strength to move in the first place.

That, and Meredith.

I'd get my own place, where no one was in charge of me but me, with open rooms and lots of sunlight and no shadows for my nightmares to hunt me from. Maybe then, the nightmares that had returned would go away, and I could build the life I wanted without having to be afraid of the dark.

"Good, it's perfect then," Meredith said, having no qualms in taking pleasure in the small act of rebellion that I was not.

I frowned. "You only met him once."

"Doesn't matter, he treated you like shit, and that's all I need to know."

I opened my mouth to say thank you, but I didn't need to. Meredith smiled and placed a hand on my arm. She already knew what I was going to say, I'd said it so many times before. I beamed as I paid for the dress.

It represented one more step forward.

I was being chased again, this time through an empty mall.

I knew it was a nightmare, but I couldn't wake myself up no matter how many times I repeated in my mind that it was only a dream. It wouldn't stop. I wanted to stop running, to sit still and tell myself it was simply another dream and that dreams couldn't hurt me. But the terror that ran up my spine and pounded on the inside of my chest and head told a different story.

It told me to keep running.

The sound of my heels clicking on the floor echoed around the empty mall. My strides were limited as I was wearing one of the dresses I'd tried on today. I couldn't see who was chasing me, so how could I know I was running in the right direction? The only thing I could judge from was the way the hairs on the back of my neck stood up and tingled and the hollow laugh that came from the shadows behind me.

But no matter which way I turned, it was always right behind me.

Running into a clothing store, I pushed my way past racks of dresses identical to the one I wore as they shifted in the non-existent wind and grabbed at my legs, threatening to tangle me up and bring me crashing to the floor. When I glanced at my feet, amongst the dresses was a tail, forked and black, edging its way through the fabric and caressing my skin.

Screaming again, I tried to stamp it away before running into the back of the shop, past the cash register desk, and into the hall lined with fitting rooms. I ran down the hall, the sound of my own panting loud in my ears. I ran for longer than should've been possible, and when I spun around, my hair falling around my face as if underwater, there was nothing but rows of doors stretching into infinity and no escape.

I chose one at random, racing in and locking the door before folding myself into the corner, curling up into a ball and gripping my hair, begging my mind to wake me up.

Because he was coming for me again.

Just as he had the night before.

He kept coming back.

Every night.

Each time he came for me, I saw a little more of him—the yellow eyes, the sharp teeth, and now a black tail. I dreaded what would happen when he was fully formed, and we were alone, trapped in my mind that refused to wake.

There was only silence and the eerie sound of my breathing echoing into space.

The sound filled my eardrums until I couldn't take it anymore and held my breath.

Silence.

Drained, tired of running, I tilted my head back against the fitting room wall. When I opened my eyes, the wall was gone, and he was behind me. My back leaned against his legs as he bared his teeth to reveal a tongue stained with blood.

I couldn't move.

He launched at me.

My eyes snapped open, and I stared at the ceiling. Hands clutching the blanket I had bunched up under my chin as though I could hide from my nightmares under the sheets. I was sweating, but my teeth were chattering. Clamping my jaw closed to stop the noise, I strained to hear anything beyond the beating of my heart and the pumping of the blood in my ears.

Somewhere nearby, someone had music on, the smooth melody indistinguishable. I could hear the refrigerator running and the traffic from outside. Clinging to these sounds of normality, I let the hum of the city bring me back into the real world, where the monsters couldn't get to me.

Where *he* couldn't get to me.

Kicking the blanket off, it tangled around my feet, and I panicked, thrashing around until it was in a pile at the end of the bed. Rolling to my side and staring at the closed curtains, a faint rectangle of light was visible around the edges from a world outside that I couldn't control any more than I could control what was going on inside my head.

I thought the nightmares had stopped when I was younger.

So, why was my attacker haunting me from every corner of this city?

CHAPTER
3

Frank

Fifteen years. That's how long I've been on Earth now.

If I were feeling melancholic, I could lean back in my office chair after a long day, rest my feet up on the desk that cost way more than it was worth, and sigh, thinking, *it seemed like only yesterday.*

Which, realistically, it did.

Because fifteen years was just a drop in the bucket of time compared to the centuries I had spent in hell. On Earth, I was a wonder boy, an example to look up to, one of the youngest CEOs the industry had seen in several decades.

Or the oldest if they knew the truth.

I took my job seriously. Of course, I did. I had to if I was to maintain the level of respect that I had come to command. If I wanted to keep myself in the lifestyle I desired, I needed to work hard because all this shit I enjoyed didn't come cheap.

Well, some of it was free.

My business partner, Mike, had been here longer than me, and I had him to thank for this life awarded to me. Mike had done everything right from the word go. He never used his powers of persuasion to get what he wanted—except, of course, to obtain the necessary identification to make it by in this world, but what choice did he have there?

On the other hand, I may have cheated a bit here and there, but who was Mike to judge? A demon was a demon and couldn't be expected to be perfect all the time. Really, I didn't know what Mike's motivations were for expelling himself from the demon life so completely. I imagined if he wanted me to know, he'd tell me, and I wasn't going to pry.

I had my theories, though.

My suspicions were it was from a bonding that went wrong and had to end, a long and painful process, which would explain the scars that dragged across Mike's back like claw marks from a deranged animal. Scars that wouldn't heal, ever.

I wondered if they still hurt him.

I cared for Mike—something I wouldn't often admit outside of my thoughts—but I respected his privacy all the same. If Mike wanted to talk about whoever she was and whatever happened, he'd talk.

For me, my motivation for leaving hell was the rules.

Rules.

How ironic that there be so many rules for demons in *hell*.

While there were still rules on Earth, I was allowed to bend and twist them until they suited my needs. As long as I didn't draw too much attention to myself, then I should be left to my own devices. The big man upstairs and his cast-down son didn't care enough to follow me to Earth, why would they? Who am I? One of thousands, millions even. If I kept my head down and didn't kill everyone who annoyed me—although it was tempting at times—I'd be left alone.

So, there were a few rules still around.

Therefore, my biggest focus after feeding my own desires was to keep the business running. Not just running but *thriving*, and all that work didn't agree with my heritage. Hard work and commitment were not words that coincided with thoughts of demons, whether people were thinking hypothetically or not.

Consequently, I needed an outlet, and sometimes sex alone didn't cut it.

So, here I was.

Rolling my shoulders, my arms shone with an uneven sheen of sweat under the dim warehouse lighting. Hours ago, I had abandoned my work shirt and shoes, having come straight from the office, and was now standing in my trousers and a tank top, my bare feet unaffected by the broken glass and sharp stones on the floor. My chest heaved as I tried to pull as much oxygen into my aching lungs as I could, the muscles in my arms flexed as I clenched and relaxed my hands a few times, preparing for the next onslaught.

Call it what you will, but it was basically a demon fight club. I'd sneer at the thought—the idea of it was ludicrous, I know—but it allowed me the release I craved. Where, even though I stayed in human form, I could unleash the worst of the inner needs and desires my body lusted after.

Violence, bloodlust, and pain—both giving and receiving.

There was only one rule—no humans.

Although I had an additional rule of my own—no marks on the face.

Mike didn't approve of such practices, and I was certain that him stamping down his inner demon with willpower alone would eventuate in an outburst sooner or later, but Mike wouldn't listen. Mike's methods simply didn't work for me. I'm not going to meditate or some shit to get through these feelings. I needed to let loose and fight the way I used to with my siblings.

Unbridled, uncontrolled, and completely unleashed.

I'd get hurt, but I would heal.

I won't be hurt as much as the demons I face.

The stranger and I circled each other. I had seen this man here before but didn't know his name or care enough to know much about him. When we came together in combat, I could feel the man's demon rippling beneath his muscles, but he was younger than me and had more faith in his fighting abilities than he probably should. He was untrained, and I was sure he was fighting purely using moves he learned from watching others, but his lack of experience wasn't my problem. If he wanted to come here and show off to his hollering friends, then I'd give them a show. I had to resist the urge to laugh, my lip curling into a sneer. I was certain the younger demon was moving with broken ribs as we circled each other. The grin broke loose on my face at the thought of the pain he'd be in, the bone grating on bone would make retaliation difficult.

If I could get him in the exact same spot again—

I was sporting several bruises and large cuts from being thrown onto the unforgiving concrete a few times. I had let him. I know it sounds arrogant, but it's the truth. My opponent relied on bulk too much and had picked me up and thrown me four times now. So, lured into a false sense of early victory, when I came at him and got under his swinging arms, I was able to break his ribs with a few well-aimed blows and move away without sustaining any further damage myself.

The small crowd jeered and hissed as our circling slowed its progress. The young demon had straightened quickly after my attack, but his face was flushed and covered in sweat, his eyes flashing with anger. A grimace plastered across his lips, cut down by the pain and a well-earned dose of humiliation. I waited, purposefully allowing myself to get too close to my opponent. Predictably, I was grabbed, and I went limp as I was thrown to the floor again. I won't pretend it didn't hurt, but I'm not a lightweight, and the act of repeatedly lifting me above his head was taking its toll.

Especially now with those broken ribs protesting with every move he made.

Rolling to the side until I was clear, I stood slowly. While the pain radiated through my shoulders, it was still worth it because it proved all I needed to know about the stupidity of the younger demon.

Too cocky.

When there were a handful of shouts of encouragement from the back of the crowd for the younger demon, he beamed and raised his arms in premature victory. I smirked at the way he winced when he lifted his arms. He was weakened.

Also, he had made another mistake.

An opening.

Rushing the other demon, I collided with his side and knocked the wind out of him in the process. Aiming for the exact spot as last time, I punched my opponent three times rapidly in the ribs, not stopping until, on the third shot, I heard that satisfying crack as another bone gave out. One more hit for good measure, I aimed with the ball of my palm in an upward motion against the broken ribs, striking with measured pressure until I saw the bone penetrate the skin. With a smirk, I struck him once more and laughed as the shattered bone shifted further until it was inches out of the shredded skin.

My opponent howled as I took aim and kicked sideways at his kneecap, the satisfying sound of him hitting the floor and the abrupt silence that followed as his friends stilled was all the confirmation I needed to know I had won. My shoulders rippled as I smelled the blood of my kin as it oozed from the younger demon's wounds and spilled onto the dirty floor. As my nostrils flared, my skin barely contained my true form, screaming to be released from its human cage and to finish what was started. It wanted to tear my opponent apart, to taste the blood, and shred flesh from bone. I rolled my shoulders again, my neck twitching as a spasm ran through my body.

No.

I wouldn't let the demon out. This victory would be enough to contain it.

For now, anyway.

Shrugging off any congratulations, my lips curled at the demons who tried to pat me on the back as I exited the circle, most of the observers parting to let me through. They could see the tell-tale signs I was grappling for control. My skin was darkening, the veins were growing black and rich, and the muscles on my face contorted as my demon relished in the violence and shifted beneath my skin's surface.

I could feel my blood surging through my veins, pumping as thick as poison and revving me up to kill. I enjoyed a fight, but I kept the instinct to kill beaten down. My time on Earth would be short-lived if I killed humans, let alone another demon and potentially exposed our kind to the human race. So, while some demons may barely walk away from the fight, while they may be crawling or dragging themselves with bloodied fingertips, they would always leave alive and retreat into hiding to let themselves heal.

After putting on my shoes, I swiped up my shirt and contemplated putting it back on until I looked down and saw my blood seeping through my tank. Best not to get blood on my shirt unnecessarily.

God, this place was making me soft.

Throwing it over my shoulder, I stalked out into the night even as I heard another fight starting behind me and let the cool air assist with my already accelerated healing.

I had to come to the other side of the city to fight and often walked home. Against Mike's advice, once he and I had become CEO's, I had partaken in several photo shoots for magazines, and consequently, was too recognizable. So, a taxi or public transportation was out as it would lead to too many questions on the off chance I was spotted by the wrong person, and a private driver would look out of place here. So, despite my clothes also being a giveaway I wasn't from this area, I walked as though I belonged, as though I had nothing to fear.

Because I didn't.

The blood on my tank and knuckles probably helped keep people at bay too.

Nobody bothered me, and if anyone looked like they were about to, they would stop the moment they saw my eyes.

Maybe for kicks on occasion, I'd allow my eyes to slide back into their natural form. Who would believe them anyway?

I was only a few blocks from having left the warehouse when I heard it.

The screams were muffled, but they were recognizably screams.

My lips curled into a scowl. I enjoyed women. Sometimes, I suppose it could be considered using them as I sought no relationship beyond the sex. But any pain I inflicted on them would be within the confines of the bedroom and completely consensual.

Even if they weren't sure they could take it, I tended to know their limits better than they did.

My smirk dropped, but I'd never rape. The sport lay in charming women, wooing them, and then bringing them so much pleasure they were literally ruined for all other men, never able to replicate what they got from me. As a low growl radiated from the base of my throat, my lip curled. The way they shuddered and screamed when I forced multiple orgasms from them even when they thought they could give no more. But I took more from them, took them until they were falling apart under me.

My cock twitched.

But rape? No.

I took particular pleasure in torturing those who were rapists once they made their way to hell. If they weren't caught and punished on Earth, they certainly were once I got hold of them.

My fists clenched, and a deep growl continued to rise in my throat as I rounded the corner into the alleyway. The muffled screams continued, but the victim and her attacker were still not visible. Rounding a dumpster, the stench of rotting garbage filled my senses and mingled with the scent of fear and the pulsation of the attacker's ecstasy in the mix.

I stilled with my arms crossed over my broad chest. The woman was lying on the ground and a man lay on top of her between her forcibly spread legs. One hand struggled to pull down his pants, and the other was planted firmly over his victim's mouth. She looked desperately over his shoulder at me, her eyes wide as the man thrust obscenely against the inside of her thigh as he worked to free himself from his clothes.

I cleared my throat.

The man barely turned his head.

"Fuck off." His voice was gruff, soaked in arousal at both the violence and impending sex and the fog of fear around the blonde woman beneath him.

I growled again. "If you like your limbs where they are, get off her. Now."

"She's a hooker. She wants it."

I shrugged. I can't say I didn't try to reason with him.

As I stepped forward, I grabbed the back of the man's collar and yanked him to his feet as the woman scrambled out from underneath him, pulling her skirt down over her shredded stockings. I rolled my eyes toward the sky as the man was exposed. "At least cover your tiny shame before I beat your face in."

"Fuck you," the man spat, struggling uselessly

against my grip.

Turning to the woman, I asked, "Was this…" waving my free hand toward the area she had been, "… consensual?"

The woman shook her head rapidly, her eyes wide.

"Cover your eyes, please," I said, trying to keep the menace from my voice that I was reserving for her attacker.

Judging by the fear in her face, I hadn't quite succeeded.

She didn't hesitate, backing further against the wall, finding a nook to hide to protect herself before covering her eyes with her palms. Something about my voice and eyes told her not to argue. I watched her, waiting until I was satisfied she couldn't see before I turned the man around to face me. His toes barely scraped the asphalt, his face was inches from mine, and I could smell the alcohol on his breath.

"So, you like to hurt women, do you?"

The man's expression shifted, his glare evaporating and fear flooding his face as my eyes changed, a flash of yellow as my hand found the man's throat and squeezed. My voice was pure darkness as I stared into the man's eyes, the light from the street glinting off my sharp teeth.

I wanted him to be afraid.

My demon was just below my skin, still hungry from the kill it was denied earlier, begging to be let out to take this human down and turn him into a blood fountain.

With my voice full of menace, I asked, "If you could keep only your dick or your balls, which would you choose?"

"Wha—"

"Choose!" The man's subsequent scream was cut off as I increased the pressure against his larynx.

He was crying openly now. "I won't do it again, I... I promise."

"I wish I could believe you." I sighed, dropping my chin as I looked back at the man. "If you don't choose, you'll simply lose them both." I let my voice take on an additional chill, allowing my demon to come to the surface just a bit more, to change my tone. The woman shivered, pressing her hands hard over her ears and keeping her eyes squeezed shut, whimpering quietly.

With a sob, he answered, and I shook him to make him speak up. He cried out, "My dick. I want to keep my dick." He finished with a heavy sob.

I had no sympathy for him.

"Very well."

With disgust written on my face, I reached down, ignoring the man's cries of "*No. Wait. Please,*" as I clamped my hand around his balls. With a twist and a jerk, my hand was flooded with hot sticky blood as the man's screams echoed throughout the alleyway and down the street. I dropped him and his decapitated testicles to the ground, leaning down to wipe my hands clean on the man's jacket. The acrid smell of the blood was in my nostrils. It smelled spoiled and diseased, and I scrunched my nose in distaste as my demon retreated, no longer interested in the taste.

Helping the woman up, I walked her around where her attacker lay and left the man there, crying in the fetal position with his hands wrapped around the bleeding wound where his manhood once was.

As we left the alleyway, the woman went to turn around to look at the scene we left behind, and I steered her forward while my hand brushed her cheek. Her hair was caked in grime from the ground in the alleyway. As she looked at me questioningly, I simply shook my head.

"Don't look."

She swallowed heavily. "Did you really just—"

"Yes. Never speak of it again." I guided her around the corner. "Where do you live?"

She pointed toward the end of the street when her voice gave out on her.

"Stop looking at me," I added sharply as we walked, and she immediately looked straight ahead, pointing to where I needed to go to guide her safely home. She had been glancing at me every few moments, taking in my features, trying to decide if she was, in fact, safe or in more danger than she was before. My jaw was taut, my demon form pressed against my skin from the inside, rippling underneath, begging to be free. The act of violence and revenge had awakened me, and now with the smell of this woman so close, it was almost pushing me over the edge.

Any good I got from the fight club was now moot.

She smelled good.

But I didn't need her memorizing my face or seeing more than she needed to. She could recognize me beyond the shattered views she was gaining from between the broken streetlights and dappled moonlight through the clouds if she kept looking at me like that. If she looked too closely, she'd see the way my veins darkened and the color spread over my skin like a bruise. I was barely containing the change and distracted myself by focusing on keeping this woman safe.

She needed my protection, not more fear. Compassion and caring weren't a part of myself I tapped into often, but that didn't mean it did not exist within me.

I wasn't a *complete* monster.

We reached her building, and I took in the dilapidated state of it, my hand twitching as I pushed gently at the small of her back, encouraging her to move forward without me. As she climbed the few stairs to the front door, I waited until she had unlocked it. She stood there awkwardly, looking at me below her on the street and biting her bottom lip.

I could see it in her eyes, she had become intoxicated by me.

I hadn't done it on purpose, but demons were sexual beings, and I had called her to me. Her eyelids were heavy as she looked down at me, her hands tugging at her clothes.

"Is there…" she swallowed heavily. I noticed the movement of the muscles in her slender neck. "Anything I can do to repay you?"

Involuntarily my eyebrows shot up. Her tone had changed, becoming thick and seductive. I knew exactly what she was offering as repayment for my saving her, but I also knew it wasn't coming from a right frame of mind. She was running on adrenaline from the attack, and on top of that, she'd been breathing in my pheromones for the past ten minutes.

Without breaking eye contact, I climbed the stairs, closing the gap between us until my chest was pressed against her breasts, separated only by the thin fabric of our clothes. She had backed away a step at my swift approach. The way I moved with purpose made her breath hitch. Whether that was with fear or excitement, I wasn't sure. Part of me didn't care. When her back hit the wall in the small porch, a squeak escaped her lips. I smiled, all teeth and lips—it was almost a cute reaction.

My shirt, wet from sweat and blood, and her dress, partially shredded from the attack, did nothing to protect either of us from our shared heat. Touching her chin, I tilted her face up to mine and silently reveled in the quiet intake of breath she couldn't control as she shivered under my touch. Her fear had been replaced with arousal at my proximity, and I sneered again, running my tongue along her jawline as she trembled.

"What's your name?"

"Evie," she whispered, her voice barely a breath against the air. Her hands were down by her sides, but she had tilted her chin and neck toward me in a silent invitation to continue.

I couldn't take her, it would be wrong, and I'd be no better than her attacker.

Beyond that, my demon was so close to the surface now, if I followed her to her bedroom, I might hurt her.

She licked her lips, and I groaned, my knees almost buckling with the test to my control.

I'd *definitely* hurt her.

Moving my lips to hers, she moaned and closed her eyes in anticipation of a kiss that never came. I slid a wad of cash into her hand, forcing it past her clenched fingers. My whisper was commanding, despite the low volume. "Make sure you have a weapon, protect yourself. If you ever get in a position like that again, don't hesitate to attack.

Because they won't hesitate to hurt you."

She released the breath she had been holding and looked at the cash, sliding it across her fingers with her thumb. I don't know for sure, but I'm guessing I handed over at least three thousand dollars. I didn't count it.

By the time she looked up, I was already down the street.

CHAPTER 4

Charlotte

His reputation preceded him. Oh boy, did his reputation precede him.

Really, they both had the same reputation, Frank Blackman and Mike Conner, successful businessmen who had worked their way up through the system from simple roots, men no one had heard of before they burst their way onto the scene. Mike first, building a reputation for his designs, but the business didn't explode until Frank came into the picture. They stormed the business world and claimed it as their own, using not only intelligence and charm, but as rumor had it, sleeping with all the right people and probably many of the wrong ones along the way.

But rumors were merely rumors, right?

These were not the kind of men you took home

to meet your parents, but definitely the kind of men you wanted to take home for the night or even a few hours.

However, all these thoughts meant I was still unsure if they were the kind of men I wanted to work for, even now as I sat in the waiting room. I had been raised by a traditional family and worked for only small family businesses before coming to the city. Hell, I could handle a joke, a harmless flirt, but would I be treated well here?

Did I have a choice?

I needed the money and would be foolish to give up this opportunity.

The doubts flickered across my mind intermittently as I took in the office space around me. Glancing at the receptionist, she was all high heels to match her high hair—nothing like me.

Was everything about this office a stereotype?

Looking at my heels, strappy but only four inches, I readjusted my position again. I had wanted to look good, but I wasn't about to risk rolling my ankle every time I stood up. I kept wondering if I could fit in here. Everything about this place was intimidating.

If given the chance, I could let my work speak for itself. I mean, I wasn't unattractive and was confident enough in how I looked. I could hold up a corporate image. Over the years, I had allowed my blonde hair to grow past my shoulders, and while the thick curls were sometimes hard to control, they were my favorite thing about my appearance. But looking at the taut hairstyles and straight hair of the women I had passed in this building, I found it was these small details that were filling me with doubt.

But Meredith told me, *fake it until you make it.*

I had done my research on Blackman and Conner—it would've been out of character for me *not* to research a business before an interview. There were no scandals associated with the company. No allegations or convictions of sexual harassment or assault, no fraud or cases of wrongful termination, and nothing to suggest their employees were unhappy or uncomfortable. So, whatever Mike and Frank did in their personal lives, they were obviously smart enough not to let it carry on into their business.

The architecture firm was now one of the largest in the state, a reminder that may as well have been plastered across the waiting room as I thumbed through one of the many magazines they left. Coming across a familiar article I recalled reading when I was working for the smaller firm back home, it had been pivotal in sparking my dreams about coming to the city.

A dream that had been kicked into high gear when I left Joshua.

Their designs were unique—*terrifying* had been

a word used to describe them more than once—but obviously terrifying in a way that also intrigued investors and clients enough to buy. They had been featured in several magazines, and it was clear they were destined for bigger things. They either wouldn't, or couldn't, tell anyone where their ideas came from, but the mixture of gothic architecture and modern lines had proven a popular one and was lined up to be the next trend to sweep the market, meaning national expansion.

This was my shot.

When I heard the door open, I turned, trying to appear as though I was casually responding to the tell-tale clack of the latch before the glass door swept across the carpeted entry. I eyed the men as they strode past where I waited for my interview. Photos were one thing, but once I saw them in person, it was abundantly clear it wouldn't take much for them to charm their way into, or out of, any situation.

It wasn't just their looks. Frank and Mike carried with them a dark aura that screamed power and something else I was less willing to admit—lust. I flushed and had to resist the urge to look away after the sly smile and lingering eye contact I got from Frank. His dark, wavy hair and darker eyes were filled with seductive promise that he could take me where no other man could.

It was clear he knew exactly the effect he had on

women, and judging by that smirk, knew the effect he had on me.

He was playing games with me already.

Scolding myself, I straightened my back. This was not the time to revert to being a teenager just because of some attractive men.

No matter how much his dark eyes made me want to touch him.

If I could just undo a few buttons, peel that shirt back.

I tutted. *Just because you've just discovered your sexual drive doesn't mean you have to let it run your entire mind now,* I had to remind myself.

This was ridiculous, a few seconds of eye contact, and I was falling apart.

Although, the voice in my head screaming for physical release was certainly a nice change from my ex's voice reminding me I was useless and *shit-house*—his words—in bed.

Sighing, I glanced at my phone before dropping it back into my large handbag—not a name brand but a cheaper knock-off.

They were running late. Not a good sign. I supposed they were used to having people wait for them, but be that as it may, it was still rude and said something about how they viewed other people's time.

Was it a power play, making me wait?

At the end of the day, this was a gateway job, one

of the best, and if it allowed me to have my own place, earn some decent money before moving on to the career I had dreamed of as an architect, then I could tolerate any kind of boss.

Feeling a smile creep across my lips, I looked at my lap. Especially one who was so easy on the eyes.

If he were the sort to play games, to taunt with the lingering effect he had, well, I could play games too.

I'd never sleep my way to the top. I wanted to work to earn it, but these men with power at their fingertips were used to winning, and I would give them a challenge—rebutting all their flirtatious jokes or smirking when they thought they had the upper hand. Maybe even let them think they had a chance.

Did that make me a bad person? Maybe. But I didn't think so. There are so many people in business who have done the wrong thing to get to the top, so what harm was it if I pretended I would, only to shut them down and step on them the way up the ladder. I'd played the game before. Hell, my casual attitude to flirtation had earned me a few shouting sessions from my ex. Not that it took much toward the end.

But he wasn't here.

Game on.

I studied the black no-nonsense writing on the wall behind the reception desk. *Blackman, Conner,*

& Associates. Bit of a mouthful, I mimed saying it as though I were answering the phone a few times to pass the seconds away.

Adjusting my dress for the seventh time in the past few minutes, I reminded myself not to take Meredith's advice again. The idea had been simple, use my resume to get my foot in the door, use my looks and a short dress to grab their attention, and use my experience and intelligence to secure the role. I had plenty of experience as a secretary and personal assistant, all within this industry, but never for such a large company. While I carried my design portfolio, I doubted they would ask or be interested to see it. Moving the papers between my fingers, I bit my lip. I was swinging wildly between utmost confidence and uncertainty about every decision I made. All the confidence I had that I was capable of this role was ebbing away with every minute they left me sitting there.

Waiting.

I sighed. After Joshua had cheated on me, it was the final straw, and I ended the emotionally manipulative relationship I had endured for years. I decided I needed a change and uprooted myself and moved away from everything I knew—the small town and my friends. I wanted the opportunity to take control of myself and my life. With no existing roots in the city aside from Meredith, who had happily offered me a place to stay, I was literally starting from scratch, and that thought was both terrifying and exciting.

But mostly terrifying.

The pay rate they were offering here was almost twice what I earned where I had previously worked. In saying that, the rent in the city was pretty much twice what I used to pay as well, but I was trying to focus on the interview and not get bogged down with details of my finances. Aside from the fact that my savings were running low, the idea of true financial independence was enticing.

But once again, my naïvety had shone through, and securing a role hadn't been as easy as I had led myself to believe it would be. My ex would say I was being reckless, that I was being emotional and wasn't thinking.

See? This is what happened. They were leaving me alone with time to think. Once I ran out of thoughts about my future plans and career and ran over my past a hundred times, I was bound to start thinking about sex again, like a goddamn hormonal teenager.

The image of Frank's eyes flashed in my mind.

I adjusted in my seat again, almost rolling my eyes at where my mind was starting to lead me.

Here we go.

"Mrs. Moore?"

I thanked God for the interruption to my train of thought as I stood. Lord help me if I got aroused while sitting in a waiting room for an important interview. "Yes, and it's Miss."

The young brunette nodded but seemed disinterested. "Follow me." She turned, her heels sounding loudly against the tiled floor. I lengthened my stride to keep up, trying to look graceful while doing so and failing, and realizing too late that every extended stride I took rode my dress further up my thighs. Glad when we reached the conference room at the end of the hall, I entered after hastily correcting my dress again as the receptionist knocked rapidly.

"Mrs. Charlotte Moore for her interview, sir."

She left while I corrected her again, "It's Miss," but she didn't look back or even acknowledge I had spoken. Apparently, taking on the additional workload as a personal assistant while they waited to fill the role didn't sit well with her, content to answer the phone and do nothing more.

"Well, she seems lovely," I muttered under my breath.

Turning back toward the man who I was hoping would be my future boss, I noticed he was smiling. I stared, sure he had overheard my sarcastic quip, but he said nothing.

As I shook his hand and sat down, I remembered not to be under any illusions about this job, despite what his easy demeanor promised. It would be fast-paced and difficult, likely with overtime and possible overnight work if I needed to travel interstate. But this is what I had dreamed of and never thought I'd take the step to achieve, and now was my time to focus on my career, and more importantly, myself.

Get out of your head and focus, woman.

"I'm Frank Blackman. I'll be conducting your interview today."

I nodded, pulling my dress down again. Frank noticed me fidgeting in my seat, and a shadow of amusement passed across his face. His eyes flickered down to the neckline of my tight dress, barely a hint of cleavage visible. I frowned as a muscle in his jaw tightened, and he clenched his teeth together when he noticed the small silver cross I wore with a simple chain around my neck.

Did he have a problem with it? Surely not.

What an odd reaction.

"You applied to be my personal assistant, correct?"

"Yes," I answered. "Sir." Mimicking the tone the receptionist had used to address him, assuming this was the protocol he requested.

His lips curved again into a small smirk. I assumed wrong. "You can call me Frank."

"Oh." I wished I didn't feel this nervous. I'd put so much pressure on myself for today and had pinpointed this as the moment where my life either flourished or failed, to make or break me.

Now I just wished he'd stop looking at me like he could see through me.

I licked my lips, my mouth suddenly dry. I was blowing it.

"Frank."

I released a breath at the look he gave me when I spoke his name, his gaze darting up from the paper in front of him to my eyes. I swallowed the urge to repeat it with a breathy whisper, enticing him to me. Feeling that familiar sensation building between my thighs, I rubbed my legs together.

Dammit.

He noticed.

His gaze shot down to my legs before making eye contact again.

Those thoughts.

Those intrusive thoughts were so strong with him I could barely concentrate.

What the fuck was going on?

I wished I'd taken Meredith up on her offer for a night out on Saturday. Maybe another one-night stand would've worked this out of my system, and I wouldn't be so nervous, constantly glancing at his arms, his chest, his jawline, and those hands.

Why *was* I so nervous?

I wouldn't deny how good-looking Frank was wasn't a contributing factor to my feelings. As cliché as it may seem, in my experience, CEOs were usually beyond middle-aged men who had let themselves go or women with stern features and tight hairdos.

But there was something else, an air about this man that made me feel as though I was coming undone by simply being close to him. He seemed to bring to the surface every feeling that tingled beneath my skin, amplifying them until I felt hot even under the cool breeze from the air conditioner vent in the ceiling.

He was watching me, almost as though he was following my thought process. That thought, in itself, was both enticing and frightening.

When he had walked past earlier and where he sat now, he moved with the easy grace of someone who had nothing to worry about. Someone who was completely confident within themselves and wanted everyone in the room to know who was in charge.

Frank was watching me, one dark eyebrow slightly arched higher than the other as he rubbed the stubble on his chin. His dark hair showed no signs of gray, although a fleck of silver could lend a hint of sophistication to his features, I decided. He looked as though he could be dangerous with the wrong expression or the wrong words. But as it were, with the slightly bemused curve to his lips, he was simply dashing.

But I reminded myself it's not like I hadn't been around or worked with handsome men before. I was supposed to be charming him with my intelligence, not by falling apart over him and his features.

I was memorizing those features with every passing moment.

Pull yourself together.

Sitting up straighter, I answered his questions as he ran through my resume and experience. I, in turn, asked all the appropriate questions and listened as he went over his expectations of the role. I didn't flinch when he mentioned the potential overtime or when he got to the wages, although that one took some willpower. His eyebrow was almost permanently arched through the interview, and I couldn't figure out if that was a good or bad thing.

He had his interview questions on a sheet of paper in front of him, which he hardly glanced at, and whenever I was answering and couldn't bear the eye contact anymore, I'd glance out the window.

But when I looked back, he was always still looking at me, studying me.

When I described my reasons for moving to the city, his lip twitched, and I was sure he was laughing at me. Rather than putting me off, this only made me more determined to prove myself to him.

A certain level of arrogance was a given with this level of power. While it didn't excuse being rude, I tried to let it run off my back, even if I'd have to punch a few pillows when I got home.

Frank stood first, and I followed quickly.

Just like that, the interview was over.

"Well, Miss Moore, you're a very promising candidate. I'll need to have a word with my associates, but we'll call you tomorrow morning to confirm."

I had to work hard to stifle my smirk as we shook hands. "Thank you for your time, Mr. Blackman." His fingers twitched in mine, and I broke out in a grin. "Frank." I straightened again, taking advantage of the way my dress curved around my chest.

His leer faltered for just a moment as his hand gripped mine, a flicker of a movement that betrayed his slip of control. I smiled, knowing I had turned it around on him, figuring that was enough payback for the look he had given me in the lobby and continued to give me throughout the interview. Although my triumph was short-lived when the feeling of his eyes raking over my body made me think of him undressing me, peeling my clothes off, and letting that gaze fall across my naked body, drinking me in.

And I wanted to *work* for this man?

Picking up my bag, I nodded at him, and he watched me leave. As I reached the door, he cleared his throat, and I turned to face him, my hand still on the handle.

"Miss Moore?"

"Yes?"

Something dark passed over his eyes, and a twitch of his hands appeared to be another momentary loss of control. "When you come in next time, maybe wear a slightly longer dress."

I flushed and nodded stiffly before leaving.

Oh, I wouldn't let Meredith forget this one.

Frank

While I dropped myself heavily into an empty seat, I watched Charlotte leave the boardroom, letting out the breath I had been holding, hissing through my teeth. Watching her leave, eyeing the way her short skirt curved around her ass and upper thighs was almost too much. I was no stranger to the female form. Obviously. But every time a woman was in front of me, physically enticing but emotionally distant, putting up a block, it set off an animalistic presence in me—a need to claim that I had to fight to keep down.

Sometimes, though, I let it out.

Charlotte was an odd one, and I was at my wit's end as to how to handle her.

On the business side of things, she seemed an excellent choice for the role. On the other hand, she seemed to constantly analyze me, trying to figure out what I was thinking, matching my every move with one of her own.

But every now and then, she'd part her lips or the way she said my name…

I grinned to myself—she was playing games with me. Whether that was conscious or not was something I'd find out. I was in no doubt that she was attracted to me, but she had strong motivations, and I didn't think she'd fall under my spell so easily.

This made her a challenge, and I was always up for a hunt.

So, while she'd be incredibly useful to have in the office, she'd also be equally as interesting to have in my bedroom. My mind flooded with images of her tied to my bed frame while I teased her until that perfect image of professionalism she seemed to work so hard to maintain came completely undone, and she was calling my name, begging me for more before she'd beg me to stop.

There was something else.

I leaned back in my chair, it groaning under my weight, and watched the empty hallway beyond the glass doors. There was something deeper, something that made my skin heat at her presence. Beyond her veil of composure and self-control, I was longing to tear apart, there was something more to her.

Mike would be pissed if I passed up on another candidate only because I wanted to leave the door open to fuck them. Sighing again, I typed up an email to HR, advising them to prepare the paperwork for Miss Moore.

Inevitably, bedding them turned out to be a mistake. None of them lived up to the expectations in my mind, and it would've been better if I had just pushed that part of me down and hired them in the first place.

Although, I felt that Charlotte wouldn't disappoint if I were to get my hands and teeth on her. She had an air about her. Not only that she had something to prove to those in her past, but something to prove to herself. Then, there was that something. That something more hiding just beneath the surface of her milky skin, as though she had hidden tendencies I could draw out of her through the meeting of pleasure and pain.

A growl crawled its way up through my throat, and my fingers froze as they hovered over the keyboard.

Tonight, I'd have to find a woman to unleash on to regain some self-control. I felt my erection pressing against the seam of my pants and shifted uncomfortably in my chair.

I would call Charlotte tomorrow and tell her the good news about her new role.

She was safe from me.

For now.

CHAPTER
5

Charlotte

Sighing loudly, I dropped my purse on Meredith's couch and drew a smirk from her.

"How did it go?" Meredith asked, eyeing me over the rim of her coffee mug with a sly smile. It was hard to be mad at her when she had that grin, a look that said she knew exactly what she had done but was just daring you to try to tell her off when she was so cute.

"Well..." I dropped one hip, my hand on my waist, trying to look stern, "... it went well, but my dress was *too short.*" I said, dragging the words and making air quotes with my fingers before pointing an accusing finger at Meredith, which did nothing except widen her grin. "And *you're* just lucky you are letting me stay here, so I can't tell you how very wrong you were."

"Yes, but..." she hooked one arm over the back of the couch as I helped myself to coffee from the kitchen, "... if you get the job, you can thank me."

I laughed. "I can thank my expertise, but thank you for your confidence in my abilities." Tugging at the dress again, I dropped my voice. "You know I'd have been expelled if I had worn something like this in boarding school."

Meredith laughed. "Maybe, but it would've been fun."

I felt an involuntary shudder down my spine—I hated that fucking school.

The reminders that crept into my life of things I wouldn't have been allowed to say or do were enough to bring the memories rushing back. My parents had sent me off without me having any say. The place was practically a monastery, strict and foreboding, no real socializing, only study and prayer. I was sure I was treated more harshly than the other girls, but then again, maybe all the students felt like that. Many of them were troubled teenagers, some who screamed in their sleep from past trauma and made me wonder what I had done to deserve being there with them.

But now, as the nightmares began to haunt me again, I dreaded the thought there was something behind them, something clawing at the inside of my mind to be remembered that would tell me I had suffered as much as they had, and maybe I did belong in that place.

I had snippets that I was weaving together, like finding all the puzzle pieces one by one. With each snippet, I remembered more of a time I didn't realize I had forgotten.

With each piece, I wasn't sure if I wanted to see the full picture.

Meredith swirled the dregs of her coffee, dissolving the last of the sugar in the mug. "So, on another note, was he hot?"

I snapped back to reality, looking at Meredith. "Who?"

Meredith raised an eyebrow, "You know exactly who. Blackman!"

"Oh," I answered while rubbing the back of my neck. I could pretend I didn't notice how good-looking he was, but it would be a lie, and I was sure Meredith would see straight through it. "Yeah. Yeah, he was gorgeous." After a pause, I added, "But arrogant as hell, like life is a big game to him."

"Earned arrogance from what I've heard."

"Perhaps, but that doesn't make it okay. Still, this position will open up other opportunities, and once I'm settled there, I can get out of your hair here."

Meredith waved her hand dismissively. "Oh please, you know you're welcome to stay as long as you need. Your family did the same for me back in the day."

"Yeah, I know, but I don't like being a burden, and

it's been three months already."

Meredith shrugged. "I can use the help with the rent. Honestly, it's not an issue."

As I sat down next to her, Meredith turned. The look on her face was a complete giveaway as to which way her thoughts were headed. I felt the corner of my mouth turn up. Meredith was clever but cheeky, and she didn't shy away from causing a bit of chaos.

"So…" she started. "Is he single?"

Laughing, I shook my head and kept my gaze stubbornly forward as I flicked the television to the news. Meredith watched me for a moment longer. I could feel her gaze but refused to look back, knowing it would result in an influx of questions about the flush creeping up my neck I couldn't hide. Meredith seemed intent on pulling me out of myself and forcing me to have fun. Which, I admitted, so far, Meredith had made being in a new city the most fun I had experienced in years. Still, I wouldn't be dragged into a conversation about my potential new boss's sex appeal. Meredith tilted her chin upward knowingly before she settled into the couch and focused on the news. The small grin that stayed on her face said she knew exactly where my train of thought was headed.

It was a bit tiring having people being able to read me so easily. Was I that much of an open book?

It wasn't long before my thoughts came back to Frank.

I had found him attractive, of course. He radiated a dark, seductive nature that would make any woman wonder not only what he looked like beneath that perfectly cut suit, but what he could do with that body. I huffed through my nose, drawing a knowing glance from Meredith, but wondering was as far as it was going to go. There had to be something more than a simple physical attraction for me to be even remotely interested in someone beyond a one-night stand, not that I had a great amount of experience in that world either.

On top of that, that's not a line I was willing to cross with an employee, let alone an *employer*. I had my future laid out in front of me, and all I had to do was keep my head screwed on, keep it in my pants, and take the opportunity with both hands.

Three days later, I strode back into the office, having been offered the position the morning following my interview and accepted eagerly. The day after my interview, I returned to complete and sign the paperwork with HR, their office being two floors below Frank and Mike's. I did this without seeing Frank at all, which probably wasn't a bad thing, as it allowed me to actually focus on the paperwork without his dark eyes watching my movements.

Since the interview, I had found it difficult to focus in general. Frank seemed to have gotten under my skin somehow, and I just hoped it was a novelty that would wear off as time passed. I hoped that with that time, Frank would become merely another co-worker who I'd say barely crossed the threshold into friendship.

After the interview, I had spent a frustrating night squirming in bed, unable to get to sleep. Every time I lay on my back and stared at the ceiling, I'd see him above me. He'd move over me, intimidating me with his body, his size, and those muscles that promised control before taking my mind and soul as he took my body. I'd part my lips to allow his kiss as I also parted my legs to invite him inside me.

I'd laid there, tossing and turning for an unsatisfying half-hour, rubbing my thighs together, until—half asleep and full of frustration—it hadn't been enough. I had allowed my hand to wander over my body and down the front of my underwear. Rubbing in small circles, I released the pent-up frustrations and buried two fingers inside my pussy, wet and ready, bringing myself to silent orgasm while biting down on my pillow.

Later, I had tried to forget that what pushed me over the edge was imagining it was his hand and fingers touching me.

I hadn't forgotten.

Frank.

There was a physical attraction, so why did I feel like there was something more? Like there was a part of this man, hidden beneath the surface, which I could only get out by running my nails down his back as he penetrated me over and over again.

How had he gotten underneath my skin so quickly as though I were under a spell? He simply oozed power, an aura about him that pulled people to him and made them eager to please him in more ways than one.

But I was stronger than this, and I was sure I could fight simple lust away. I had not uprooted my life and moved to the city to get caught up with the first man who gave me butterflies.

My relationships had been few, but both were long-term. My first, Cole, ended when he was forced to move away before our final year of college. We tried to make the long-distance thing work, but as is the old story, it failed. He met someone else but was honest with me before he pursued it, and I gave him my blessing, keeping my tears at bay until I hung up the phone. It had been far from easy letting him go, but it was the right thing to do.

I could hear it in his voice, his longing for this

other woman, how his passion for me had died as the miles stretched out between us and tore us apart. I stalked him on social media now and then. He had married that woman, and while I wished them all the best, there was always that flush of jealousy in my stomach at the thought of what could've been.

After Cole, Joshua had been everything I thought I needed. I had turned down his advances for long enough to convince myself that my interest in him was more than simply a rebound. But as our years together stretched on, I started to feel constricted, eventually listening to my instinct that something was wrong. My parents were angry at me when I left him. To them, a woman was nothing without a partner to become a husband and have children to raise. They didn't care about the emotional trauma. As far as they were concerned, he was only being protective over me like a good man should be. I had never figured out if they were blind to the truth or simply chose to ignore it.

I heard somewhere that your family was like your shadow, meaning they were always there with you. But I didn't realize this meant they disappeared when things went dark.

Joshua had kept me in the darkness for so long, barely allowing interaction with men other than him, keeping a close eye on co-workers and ruining more than one friendship. Until it wasn't only men, but one by one, all the people in my life were pushed away. Perhaps, this is why Frank was having such a strong effect on me. He represented everything that was the opposite of Joshua—freedom, liberation, sexual chemistry.

Perhaps I couldn't logic my way out of this.

"What are you doing?" Frank asked, striding down the hallway toward me and pulling me from my thoughts. I'd stopped and was just about to drop my handbag under the reception desk in the expansive foyer.

Frowning for a moment, I cleared my expression before I answered, "Just putting my bag down."

"You're not working here." He pointed down the hall. "Your desk is outside my office."

"Oh, okay. Sorry, I didn't know."

Frank approached me as I came back into the main foyer, closing the gap between us when I expected him to move away and show me to his office. I almost walked into him, pulling myself up before I collided with his chest.

Being close enough to trace the outline of his chest muscles through his shirt, I raised my eyes to his as he bore down on me. I refused to shrink under that gaze because I didn't like what I saw in it.

"Did you misunderstand your role?" His tone was condescending, but the backdrop to his tone only confirmed what I thought I saw in his face.

It sounded like hope.

He was *hoping* I misunderstood, *hoping* I didn't want to be here.

I frowned at him in earnest, not bothering to hide the expression. Why would he want me to fail? Why hire me if he didn't want me here?

He was so close I was sure my breasts would brush his chest if I breathed too deeply. Subconsciously, I rolled my shoulders forward, trying to flatten my breasts away from touching him.

Not because I was uncomfortable, but because I *wasn't* uncomfortable and knew I should be.

I wasn't sure I could take that sort of intimate contact with him, not after the thoughts that penetrated my mind when I was alone in bed the other night.

"No, no, that's completely fine," I said, determination in my voice.

We stared at each other for way too long.

Frank

Looking down at where our bodies nearly met, I was annoyed at myself for allowing hope to flare inside me a moment earlier. If she failed at this job or didn't want it, then there'd be nothing holding me back from bedding her, and with nothing to hold me back, I'd ravage her.

I would *destroy* her.

The thought had made it into my mind long enough for it to decimate all the control I had built up after the interview, all the mental work I had done to push her firmly into the role of employee and nothing further.

Those walls had crumbled when I had moved too close.

My fault. But it was like being pulled with an invisible force, my willpower only coming into play in the last inches before I was pressed against her.

From the way her chest heaved and her breath hitched, I knew it wasn't just me.

That made it worse.

Plastering an award-winning smile on my face, I pushed the intrusive thoughts from my mind and reminded myself how Mike would react if I screwed up another chance of a reliable employee because of my animalistic desires.

Look at me, Mike would say, *I can control myself, why can't you?*

I grinned. "Better than fine, I hope," I said after her clipped response. I stayed next to her for a beat longer than necessary before turning and leading her to my office.

CHAPTER 6

Charlotte

Wanting that extra distance, I watched him walk away for a moment before I followed.

Needing that extra distance.

What was that all about? Was he messing with me? Did he treat all staff like this? I recalled the disinterest he had shown when speaking to the receptionist and the business-like tone he had used when communicating with HR when I signed my contract. He had phoned them from his office to clear up some details about the role, and his voice was clear from where I sat across the narrow desk. There was none of that dangerous darkness to his voice, no seduction in the tone.

So, whether he realized he was doing it or not, it was just with me.

Who was I kidding? Of course, he knew he was

doing it. A man like Frank Blackman doesn't lose control.

Although, it was tempting to find out if I could make him do it, to push him hard enough.

Obviously, whatever it was that had sparked inside me during the interview wasn't entirely one-sided.

I could play the game, be friendly and flirt. Why not? It might even help to release some of the tension I've been holding onto.

But I sure as hell wasn't going to risk this career opportunity in exchange for sex.

Frank

After I showed Charlotte around and we reached her desk just outside the glass door to my office, I pulled the chair out for her. She looked at me and returned my smile, but my polite gaze turned into a smirk when I could see that hers hadn't been entirely genuine, more of a social reflex. She was sizing me up, trying to figure out who I was while still keeping up barriers between us.

I liked this game, and I liked that she thought she could play as well as me.

I'd make her work for every inch of who I was.

Watching her intently as she settled into her chair, she then immediately reached down and adjusted the back tilt, making the space hers, claiming it. It was a small gesture but didn't go unnoticed. Along with the tiny adjustments of the angle of the monitor, keyboard, and phone, they all added up to a clear statement—*this is my space.*

I imagined she wouldn't wait for more than a day or two before she had a trinket on her desk, maybe a photo. Would it be of a boyfriend? I felt a flame of jealousy burn within me, which I worked to put out quickly. Not only was I making judgments on situations I didn't know the answer to, but I was also getting protective over a woman I had met only once before.

Here I was, trying to justify the reasons for my feelings of protectiveness toward her, or perhaps a more suitable word—possessiveness. She was independent or at least appeared to be. It seemed she had thrown herself into an unfamiliar situation to force herself to stand on her own two feet, to rid herself of the constraints placed on her by expectation.

I respected that. In a way, it mirrored my story.

But there must have been something else. These were not traits that I hadn't encountered in women before. I was keen to peel back the layers that made Charlotte who she was and figure out exactly what was so enticing about her—to find what it was that had my demon scratching at the inside of my body, demanding to be closer to her.

Not that I disagreed with that side of me.

Inhaling deeply as I stood behind her, I had to resist the urge to bend forward and hover my lips above her collarbone and breathe in her scent. Again, I noticed the tiny cross that dangled just above the enticing lines of her breasts. She didn't have the feel of someone who attended church regularly. Religion was hardly kryptonite to demons, but it certainly left a visible aura and scent on the humans who practiced often. Charlotte didn't have this, so the cross was either purely for decoration or a relic of religion left behind.

Interesting.

Running her through the workings of the phone system, she nodded politely. But while she stayed silent during my tutorial, letting me talk and nodding at me with her eyebrows raised, whenever I paused to check she was following, I quickly realized she didn't need me here.

Too bad.

This was all standard procedure, but with Charlotte, I felt like I was holding her back from something more important. I cleared my throat as I handed her a pile of reports I needed entered into the system, she took them and turned her chair to face her monitor before I had even made a move to my office.

She was sending me a message.

I don't need you to babysit me.

I'm not stupid. I knew exactly what her physical cues were telling me, but I have never responded well to being told what to do, even if it was delivered in a subtle social cue. I stood my ground behind her for no reason other than to make a point.

Charlotte

The heat coming off Frank as he stood behind me was overwhelming, his eyes boring holes into the back of my head. I had been keen to get to work, hoping it would offer a suitable enough distraction from his masculine form so close. Hoping I had sent him a strong enough hint that I didn't need to be watched through the simplest of tasks, I opened up the system with the login provided in the email from IT and started punching in the data. I'd used this system before, knew my way around it, and I could concentrate and get things done.

If only he'd leave.

His proximity became distracting, and my fingers hesitated as they flew across the keyboard. I had to resist the urge to turn and tell him he didn't need to stand there, but he seemed to want to watch me work for a moment, for whatever reason. Closing my eyes and inhaling deeply, I was distracted again. He smelled so good—subtle spices of dark cologne.

Fuck.

I breathed a sigh as he walked around from behind my desk. My eyes followed him as he moved into his office and sat—the view of his desk was clear through the large glass doors.

Great, that wouldn't be distracting or anything.

Quickly, I glanced away as he looked at me but not before seeing that shadow of a smirk on the corner of those perfect lips.

This wasn't going to be as easy as I thought.

CHAPTER
7

Charlotte

Gathering the empty water bottles from the boardroom table, I tossed them in the bin in the corner of the room, resisting the urge to attempt a few different trick shots. The only result of that would be me failing the shots and embarrassing myself in the process. It had been two weeks in this job, almost to the day, and I was still trying to keep my interactions with Frank limited and professional, which was working.

Most of the time.

He seemed to be spending as much time sizing me up as I was him. I had caught him smiling at me more than once but had also found out a few things about him, including that he shared my sense of humor. He'd make passing comments that made me laugh, and I could always entice a grin from him in return with my responses.

None of this was helping my resolve.

The more I tried to stay away, the closer I wanted to be.

On the odd moments we were physically close, I could almost feel him resisting the urge to touch me.

Unless, of course, that was just me trying to justify my urge to touch him.

"Can I help?"

I looked up to find Frank leaning against the door frame, his shirt was untucked, and he had discarded his suit jacket.

"You let yourself go quickly." I smiled. "The second the meeting is over and the clients are out the door, you ruin your suit."

Frank looked down and spread his arms with a smirk. "I'm all about comfort."

Walking around the table toward him, I picked up a handful of wrappers along the way. I'd never understood businesses' obsession with mints or why people consumed so many during meetings. Was it just because they were there? Because they couldn't stand to sit still for that long and pretend they were paying attention? Or was it to keep them awake while they thought about what they would be doing as soon as this was over?

"That's a lie." I continued, "You're all about appearance."

As I got closer, I hesitated, then looked at the clock on the wall and tutted. It was only two in the afternoon. "The workday isn't over yet," I muttered, my need for control and professionalism pushed aside my hesitations as I straightened his shirt. He was the CEO, for God's sake, he needed to take more care of himself.

When he didn't protest but instead straightened his shoulders and shifted his arms slightly away from his body so that I had better access, I tugged his shirt taut and tucked it in. When my fingers grazed against the V-shape of his muscles through the thin fabric of his tank, an arrow pointing my attention down to where I shouldn't be looking, I tried desperately to ignore the touch. But I felt his stomach shrink away from my hands and heard his intake of breath, a small gasp that I found myself wanting to turn into a moan.

Fuck, fuck, fuck, fuck.

Frank

"Sorry, my hands are always cold," Charlotte said with a broken laugh.

"S'okay," I whispered, my voice hitching.

Her hands weren't cold. That's not why I stuttered.

I held my breath and watched her fingers, my

skin tingling with the memory of where she had been so close to touching me. She continued to busy herself fixing my tie, but when she raised her eyes to mine, the smirk dropped from her face, and I saw the realization of just how close we were as it dawned on her.

She released a shaky breath and took a step away from me. The space between us turned cold as I longed for the warmth of her back against me. I stared at her, daring her to come closer again, close enough for me to wrap my arms around her and hold her still.

Because I could make her be still.

"Much better," she said, averting her gaze from me and looking back at the boardroom. "You can start by wiping the table down." She walked around the table and tossed a cleaning rag at me.

I caught it with one hand, having barely paid attention to its trajectory as my eyes followed only her. "You're seriously going to make me clean?"

She looked amused and shrugged. "You offered."

"It was obviously an empty offer to make me seem friendly, which you were supposed to turn down."

"Don't worry, I won't tell anyone your secret."

"Which secret is that?"

She glanced at me, a look that always seemed to say *I'm on to you.*

If only she knew.

"The secret that you're actually nice." After a beat, she added, "So, what brought you to the city?"

I shrugged. "Freedom, power." I displayed my devilish grin, the one I knew she knew meant I was playing with her. "Women."

But she didn't respond to the comment.

"Freedom from what?"

I paused. She had smiled at my obvious bait but then asked a question I hadn't expected. Apparently, her way of sizing me up was more direct than my usual games. "From rules." I sighed before grinning again. "I wanted to make my own rules."

Charlotte stopped cleaning and looked at me. "That actually sounded like an honest answer."

I shrugged again, my lips still playing with a shadow of a smile, pleased with myself for turning her game into mine. "Not sure why you sound so surprised."

She laughed. "Because you're always *on*. I just get the feeling that you're always putting up a front."

"You haven't known me that long."

"Long enough."

"This is who I am."

"Liar," she muttered, still smirking and going back to cleaning.

She has no idea.

"What about you?" I asked.

"Came here for a fresh start and to begin a true

career, not just a job."

"So, you're just using me as a stepping stone?"

Her expression was coy. "That depends how this goes. I'm not going to pretend I'm not looking at advancement, but I'll work for it." At my silence, she continued, "I can't be the only one."

"The only one who used me and not just for my banging body?"

Charlotte tutted and shushed me as I chuckled. I knew there was a smile hidden behind the hair that fell in front of her face. She was an odd one, there were only a small group of women who didn't fall victim to my charms immediately and an even smaller part of that group that I had the urge to chase. I could feel the heat from her in response to being this close to me, but she was fighting it, whether purely through a professional obligation to keep a distance or something else, I wasn't sure.

The irony of her telling me that I put on a front wasn't lost on me. I wanted to bring out whatever it was that *she* was hiding. It seems she, too, was an expert on that.

She was career-focused but young and beautiful enough to find a rich partner and never have to work again, and I wasn't quite sure why she didn't take advantage of that. I came to Earth for fun, working through necessity, but if she didn't have to work, then why would she?

Charlotte

The conversation flowed easily between us, and with every moment that passed, I felt Frank being less of the person he was trying to portray and more of the person he actually was. Behind every dirty joke, even if I secretly enjoyed the crudeness of his humor, and every display of arrogance was someone who didn't usually get a chance to talk openly.

I found I liked the man behind the mask, a pleasant surprise given his arrogant and domineering exterior, but I was still distracted by every brush of his fingers on the back of my hand when we passed something between us.

As Frank crossed the boardroom to finish putting the catering supplies away, he moved slower than necessary. His strides were usually confident and strong, and he walked fast. Perhaps he had enjoyed my company as I had his.

Because when I sat back at my desk outside his office, I was his assistant again, rather than two people enjoying their time together.

As we came to a bottleneck in the room between the large table and wall, I froze when he passed behind me, failing to stop myself from gasping. But Frank noticed. He noticed the breathy intake when my ass brushed against his groin. He noticed the way I froze, and I could almost feel the grin on his face without needing to see him. He leaned forward and stopped, his lips inches from my neck.

"You smell nice."

I chuckled breathlessly. "That's creepy."

"I'm a creepy guy," he drawled, making me laugh again. He chuckled when I gasped, chastising myself for not having better control over my responses.

But I didn't, not around him.

He moved his hips forward, ever so slightly against me. The movement was so small, it could've been an accident, but I knew better. Instead of pulling away and telling him where to shove it, it took all my willpower not to press back against him.

My knuckles turned white as I gripped the chair in front of me, the leather creaking against my grip.

He knew.

Frank wouldn't have dared make a move like that unless he knew how I felt around him. He was tempting me, calling me to him.

He chuckled quietly then moved past me. "Well, looks like we're done." As he left the room, he added, "It was nice talking to you, Charlotte."

"You, too..." I replied, an unnatural smile plastered on my face, which I hoped was successfully distracting from the flush that covered my neck at the feel of him touching me, wishing it were more, "... Frank."

"This isn't okay, Meredith."

"What's the problem?"

Meredith was sitting on the couch watching me as I paced the room before I stopped and rounded on her. "I'm like..." I waved my hands around, searching for the words, "... weirdly attracted to him."

"But he is..." Meredith mimicked my hand motions, barely containing her glee, "... weirdly attractive."

"He's my *boss*, and this isn't okay. I took this job for a purpose. I have plans! But he's so distracting."

"Well, the way I see it, you've got three options."

I dropped myself onto the couch, huffing, "What?"

"You can quit."

"What? No."

Meredith held up her hands, counting the options off after my protest. "You can just tolerate the tension, or you can fuck him," she ended, shrugging.

"T-those are all terrible options," I stuttered as I stared at her.

Meredith shrugged. It wasn't a dismissal of the

conversation but more an acknowledgment that she didn't know the solution to the problem. We sat in silence for a moment, each lost in our thoughts.

Meredith patted her hand on my leg. "Show me the apartments you're looking at."

Flicking my fingers across the laptop mousepad, the screen came to life. I pointed, and Meredith made the appropriate sounds of appreciation. When she asked to see the next one, and I didn't respond, she looked up and watched the indecision I knew was plastered on my face.

"I'm having nightmares, Meredith," I whispered.

"The ones from your childhood?" she asked as I nodded. "Are they the same ones?"

"Not quite," I mumbled. I wasn't entirely sure I wanted to get into this conversation and voicing it would make it real.

"When did they start again?"

"When I moved to the city."

I stilled as the laptop screen went black again. If I let my eyes lose focus, staring into the black window, I could almost see a face. I could just about make out details that I couldn't quite remember, hidden in the recesses of my mind behind all the nightmarish imagery that came to the forefront every other night.

Once Meredith had asked when the nightmares first started, the truth was I wasn't quite sure. I couldn't remember if it was before or after I went to boarding school, if I was at my parents' house when the images first came to haunt me, or if I had woken one night in that dark school, sweating and panting and wishing I had someone to hold me and take the darkness away.

When I stared at the screen, a face started to form. At first, it was just eyes, then teeth. Then those eyes turned yellow, stark against the black backdrop.

I slammed the laptop shut.

"Is there anything I can do to help?" Meredith asked, watching my face much too closely.

When I shook my head, I intentionally let my hair fall in front of my face. I regretted starting this conversation. It was no reflection on Meredith, but I wanted to hide as much as I could. Yet every day, the images came back clearer. "No, I think it might just be stress."

"Is it your job?"

"It's everything, I think. The job, finding a new apartment, being in a new city." I sighed. "My boss."

"We're back to Frank again."

"We're never *not* back to Frank, he's on my mind constantly. He's taken up residence in my brain and won't get out." I looked at Meredith, pleading with my eyes for her to solve all my problems for me. "This is possibly the most inconvenient way to meet a man that I'm *this* attracted to." Running my hands over my face, I mumbled into my palms, "I love my job, and I don't want to do anything to ruin that."

"So don't." Meredith rubbed my back in small circles as I leaned forward, pressing my face into my hands and my elbows on my knees. "He's just a man. I'm sure it'll pass. Sounds like lust to me."

I let my hands fall to the couch, leaning back and asking the ceiling, "How can someone even *be* that attractive? It's not human."

Meredith laughed. "I don't know, but your imagination is going to have to be where it stays."

CHAPTER

8

Charlotte

As the weeks stretched out, I cemented my position in the firm. I had made several valuable contacts in other businesses, two of whom had already more than subtly suggested that they would have a position waiting for me if I ever chose to move on. Of course, I hadn't told Frank about these proposals, not wanting him to overreact or burn my bridges here.

Or perhaps I'd keep them to myself in case I needed them as ammunition for a future promotion.

Since I started, Frank had maintained a steady level of flirtatious behavior with me. I was surprised that other people in the office didn't have more of an issue with his overly open approach, he certainly made his intentions clear. While his reputation with women was not unknown, from chatting with co-workers, I had learned that he usually kept it outside the office, keeping his work and play separate.

Sure, he'd make the occasional comment, but it was harmless, and not once did any of his female employees feel pressured or uncomfortable.

So why was it different with me? Why had it escalated beyond that? I was nothing special. I'm sure every woman he came across reacted to him the way I did.

But the way *he* reacted to *me*?

While I had enjoyed the casual friendship I had formed with Frank beyond the employer-employee relationship, there were a handful of things about Frank I couldn't figure out.

One of those was the string of strange clients who came into his office on an almost weekly basis. I got to know the characters but never their names. They never made appointments or called ahead and never introduced themselves to me. I'd watch them as they walked past me into Frank's office, striding through as if they owned the place. I had access to all of the accounts and knew there was nothing shady going on in the background. So why Frank kept company with such people must be personal, at least to an extent.

The first time one of them had come in, I had nicknamed him Damien because he reminded me of the creepy child from *The Omen*, with his dark hair and empty eyes. I had asked if he had an appointment as he went to walk past me, then stood when he ignored me and repeated my question with more authority in my voice.

As much authority as I could manage while he made my skin crawl.

He had rounded on me, approached me with the same confident strides he had entered the offices with, and backed me against the wall. He made a sound I could only describe as a snarl as he breathed in, and the noise echoed in the back of his throat as he gazed at me the way a predator assesses its prey. His face was close to my neck, sending another shiver down my spine. My arms were pinned behind me against the wall, he was so close any movement would make me touch him, so I stayed still. As I stretched my face away from him, and the hair on my arms and back of my neck raised, I did the only thing that seemed to come to me naturally.

I growled at him.

Not sure where it had come from, it had simply worked its way from the bottom of my throat as naturally as if I had done it a hundred times before. He had drawn back in surprise before a menacing sneer grew on his face, and he boxed me in with his arms, opening his mouth to retaliate. His teeth were too close to my throat, threatening to rip it out.

He was going to tear my throat apart. I told myself it was a ridiculous thought, but his eyes told me otherwise.

"Back up!"

Damien and I had both looked up at Frank's command. His fists were clenched, the muscles in his tense arms visible with his sleeves rolled up. A muscle twitched in his jaw. I don't recall seeing him that angry before. When Damien didn't move, Frank covered the floor with a handful of strong strides, grabbed Damien by the back of his t-shirt, and wrenched him away from me.

Breathing a sigh of relief as my space was no longer invaded by Damien, whose mere proximity made me uncomfortable, a feeling of fresh air swept around me the instant he was moved. I tried to shake the murderous look in his eyes from my head. Unsuccessfully.

"Don't go near her again," Frank ground out through gritted teeth.

Damien merely smiled. "Let me go, Frank, unless you want me to sit out here and talk to her all day."

Frank let him go, thrusting him away with force. Damien regained his footing and swaggered back toward Frank after his stumble, a grin still on his face. "Got a minute to spare for an old friend?"

Barely containing my shock when Frank nodded instead of throwing him out, Frank led the way into his office. He threw me a look that simply said, *don't ask,* and I slowly sank back into my chair.

Tapping my pen impatiently against the stack of paper in front of me, I wasn't achieving much and kept biting my lip as I glanced at Damien and Frank. They spoke for only a few moments before Damien had swept out of the office, a smirk on his lips.

This morning another such customer was in Frank's office, without an appointment as usual, but somehow allowed to bypass the rules that keep other clients in check and with the respect Frank deserved. This one I just called the Tall Man, for obvious reasons. Tall and willowy, he walked as though he was going to sweep his arms out to the side and grab people from around him. I could imagine him pulling someone into his embrace and squeezing the life from them like a boa constrictor.

I wasn't sure why Frank's *friends* sent such thoughts into my head, but I couldn't escape them. Every one of them had the feel of a nightmare living in human skin.

Looking up from my computer as I heard a shout from the office, I stood abruptly when the yelling continued. I wanted to help but knew I wasn't supposed to go into Frank's office when he had visitors—clients and personal alike. Hovering on the edge of indecision, I jumped when the office door crashed open, and the man left with Frank shouting obscenities at his retreating back.

I hesitated for only a moment longer before I

trotted into his office. "Mr. Blackman... Frank... is everything okay?" I had heard him argue with clients before but not like that.

Frank roared and punched the wall, leaving a crater of dust and plaster.

"I'm not a bad man!" he growled.

I jumped, and an involuntary squeak escaped my lips. Embarrassing, but there it was. I clamped my hands over my mouth as he rounded on me. Unable to tear my eyes from his as the rage flickered across them, his shoulders heaved with each arduous intake of breath.

He was terrifying, a dangerous force barely contained by his physical form.

He was beautiful in his rage.

"I, uh..." I stuttered. "I'll leave."

"Miss Moore."

Stopping mid-step after turning to leave, my back still faced Frank, I hunched my shoulders against the daggers hitting me from the intensity of his gaze. When I faced him, his expression had softened. Glancing between him and the hole in the wall, I decided it was better to maintain eye contact with him than be too obvious in my noting of the way the bricks behind the plaster had dented and cracked.

"I'm sorry," he offered. "Did I scare you?"

"No," I answered too quickly. He raised his eyebrows. "Yes... no." I sighed. "A little bit."

I took a few steps toward him, gaining confidence as I got closer. He stood still, waiting for me to come to him, barely moving as though he'd scare me off. Like I was a deer, and he was a waiting mountain lion, only ready to pounce when I got too close. When I drew level with him, I lifted his hand and inspected his knuckles, whispering, "Are you okay?"

He twitched as though he were going to pull his hand from my grasp. "I'm fine."

"Can I ask what happened?"

Frank didn't move. He was watching my fingers run across the back of his hand. A gentle gesture I didn't even realize I was doing.

What was this? He obviously knew I was attracted to him, but he looked uncomfortable at the concern swimming in my eyes. "He wanted a favor. I didn't want to give it."

"Are they friends of yours?"

"Something like that."

"Why don't you just tell him no?"

"It's not that simple."

To gain additional information, I wanted to ask more, but didn't want to overstep. His answers were clipped. If he wanted me to know, he'd tell me. I had no claim over this man. "Shall I tell him he's not allowed in if he comes again?"

Frank's expression contorted. "No. Let him in. It would be dangerous for you to confront them.

Leave them to me."

"But—"

"Please stop asking questions." He pulled his hand from mine. "That will be all, Miss Moore."

I left the office, but the dismissal felt more like a rejection.

CHAPTER 9

Frank

Charlotte smiled and looked up as my shadow crossed her desk. "Good morning, Frank."

"Good morning, Miss Moore."

"I call you Frank because you asked me to, so when are you going to call me Charlotte?"

Quirking a brow involuntarily, I mused. I had ideas in my head of the scenario as when I'd call her Charlotte, so I opted not to answer but simply continued to grin at her. A frown cast over my face when she held her hand out, palm up over the desk. She watched me with an arched eyebrow, waiting with her hand held out expectantly. I didn't know what she wanted. When I didn't move, she snatched my right hand and inspected the knuckles.

"Fast healer," she commented.

My smile faltered. "It wasn't that bad." I glanced

at my office.

Noticing my gaze, Charlotte said, "I've already booked in the plasterer to fix the wall." Her tone was all business again.

"What did you tell them happened?"

She shrugged. "They didn't ask, and I didn't tell."

I watched her. She was stroking the back of my hand with her thumb again. She followed my gaze and paused, confirming my suspicions that she didn't realize she was doing it. Yesterday and now. The way she had looked at me yesterday had thrown me, and my instant reaction had been to shut off. It wasn't a look of lust or desire but genuine concern.

It was too much.

Mumbling an apology, she let go of my hand. I hesitated before knocking her desk twice with my knuckles—a gesture of nervous energy that made me feel as ridiculous as it looked—so I turned to walk away.

Charlotte

He stopped and spun back to my desk. "Miss Moore?"

"Yes?" I had returned to typing but looked up with a clear expression as I answered, hoping he hadn't noticed the way I flinched when he spoke and took a beat of time before responding. The way I touched his hand had startled me, the way it felt so comfortable, so natural. On the spot, I decided I would try harder to keep my relationship with Frank strictly professional. I was going to take a figurative step back, and any signs of affection or attraction I'd push down and ignore.

Yep, I had made that decision all right.

But then again, I had made that decision at least a dozen times since I started this job. The resolve was wiped from my mind every time I saw him.

This jumble of contradicting thoughts was hard for me to take. I was usually so clear-minded and organized. Save for the nightmares, my mind was a structured office in itself.

But he, he tore it down every time.

I'd scold myself later for the way I had touched him.

"I'm sorry if I scared you yesterday."

I pressed my lips together. "I'm sorry you were made to feel that angry." Then beamed before adding, "Would you like me to beat them up for you, Mr. Blackman?"

He laughed that fucking laugh. "No, thank you…" he smiled before pausing, "… Charlotte."

When he said my name, he looked at me with such significance, and I knew. As if I didn't already know, but it was cemented then.

I was in so much trouble.

Frank

Shortly after the too-emotional exchange, I decided I was going to pretend it didn't happen, so I walked past her desk again and dropped a file on her keyboard. She pushed it to the side resolutely with the pen she kept tucked between her thumb and forefinger while she continued to type and finished the sentence in the report she was working on—a proposal for a building that would add to the already iconic city skyline. As she hit each key with purposeful precision, I grinned, watching her. I knew she could touch type, but she was making a point, trying to put me in my place.

She was trying to reform the boundaries we had crossed already.

I'd love the chance to put her in her place.

On her knees in front of me.

Slowly and resolutely, she turned, took the file I had dropped, and flipped through it, intermittently glancing up at me under her lashes. I swallowed back another urge that flared inside me—that glance only reaffirmed the image in my head of her on her knees.

I watched her move. She was so desperate to appear in control, she raised her eyebrow delicately at the right places as she read, but my senses were heightened to her. I noticed the slight tremble in her hands, the way her fingers missed the edges of the pages as she flipped through the file and hurried to correct herself, and the brush of skin on skin as she moved a stray hair from her face and tucked it behind her ear.

It was me. I affected her.

Of course, I knew that. I'd known it since the day I saw her waiting in the foyer for her interview. She was trying to hide it. But every twitch, every hitched breath, told a story to me of a human woman trying to maintain control when all she could think of was tearing my clothes off. Or have me tear *hers* off.

I fought back my urge to grin. My internal battle raged—not that I had been hiding it as she was—because I obviously wanted her too. She'd be holding back to protect her career. I was holding back for the same reason, and perhaps more so to protect her from me. Because with the effect she had on me, with whatever it was that drew me to her, I wasn't sure that given the chance to take her I'd be able to contain my demon.

There were moments when she looked at me with an almost tender look. I desired to spank her until that look came off her face and show her that tenderness and Frank Blackman didn't belong together.

With her, I didn't see a one-night stand. I saw many nights and days lost in each other's embrace and a tangle of sheets. That much intimacy and I'd definitely lose control.

I shifted uncomfortably, and Charlotte's eyes were drawn to me at the movement.

"Conference?" she asked.

"Yep, and you're coming."

"Why?"

I cocked an eyebrow at her. "Do you always question your bosses?"

She looked sweetly at me. "I always question everyone."

"That's a lie." I smirked. There she goes again, always wanting to be in control.

I could show her what control really means.

"Because it's about networking, making a good impression. Finding new talent, new technology. I've been impressed with your work, and I want your insight, your organization..." my gaze shifted slightly, "... and your image to represent us."

Her look was coy, and I was forever thankful that she took my humor for what it was—harmless.

Mostly.

"I'm not a display piece, Frank."

"I want your expertise."

She closed the file. "Leave it with me. I'll get the flights and accommodations booked."

"Make sure our rooms are close together, so I can keep an eye on you and keep you out of trouble."

I chuckled as her control faltered, her jaw

dropped, and a flush crept up her neck to her cheeks.

"We fly out next week." And with another cheeky grin that made her resolve slip and her legs shift, almost subconsciously welcoming me, I went back into my office.

Because I had noticed that shift of her legs, I needed to sit down to hide the growing hardness barely contained in my slacks. My reasons for wanting her at the conference were truthful, but how I'd make it through without taking her was something I was still figuring out.

CHAPTER
10

Charlotte

Day one of the conference was over.

While I stood at the hotel bar, I shifted my weight between my feet uncomfortably before giving up and sliding onto the bar stool. I hated these damn stools, they were always too tall for me, and I had to sit with my feet tucked under me and on the small footrest, trying not to look like a child in an adult's world.

Having expressed this hatred to Frank, he tossed his jacket onto the bar and ordered a drink for himself and a top-up for me. He laughed a genuine laugh that made the skin around his eyes crinkle in a way I loved. It took away from the serious resting expression he usually had that darkened his features. I watched as his eyes did the casual sweep of my legs in those stockings, taking in the black heels and ending at the glimpse of lace at the hem of my skirt.

"You don't look like a child but a woman to me," he growled out.

Pulling my skirt down slightly, the gesture didn't do much good with my legs tucked under the stool the way they were. Once again, I was reminded how I hated my thighs. When the thigh-gap thing became a craze, I didn't wear jeans for months and still rarely did, as my thighs had always rubbed together. Meredith had said I was curvy, Joshua had said I was fat, and I knew which one I believed.

But watching the way Frank drank in my appearance every morning, I was starting to believe Meredith may be the right one.

Swirling my drink, I looked down at my hands. "Is it always like this?" I whispered.

"Like what? The conference?"

"No," I ran my finger around the rim of my glass, waiting for it to ring the way the glasses did in my parents' house, stopping when I remembered those were their best crystal. I sighed. "I mean with your assistants, the way you look at me, the playful flirting. Is it always like this with all women?"

I wasn't sure if I was jealous of the prospect or what I expected him to say. Did I want to hear that it was the same with everyone? Would that take the pressure off and ease the tension if I knew I was only one of many? Or would it make it feel worse?

I was used to flirting without any intent behind it. But somewhere along the line, it had changed with Frank, and I suspected it may have been as early as my first day. We were drawn to each other in a way I hadn't been with anyone before, and while I should be pushing him away and demanding he stop, I really wanted him to go further, and that frightened me.

Because if this was something, really something, was it worth giving up over a job?

"How many drinks have you had?" He looked amused.

"This is my third."

"Ah, and we're already into the deep end."

I looked at him, and the smile never strayed from his lips. If he was uncomfortable at my having asked, he didn't show it.

"Do you want the honest answer or the professional one?" he questioned.

"Honest. Of course."

He drummed his fingers on the bar. "No, it's not always like this."

Nodding, I finished off my drink without looking at him as he watched me with his head tilted before sighing and sitting next to me.

"Charlotte." I looked up as he spoke my name and watched him watch me. He put his hand on the bar, and it almost seemed like it was an abandoned attempt to take mine. "There's something about you, and you have no idea how hard it was for me to decide to hire you."

"Why? Did I do something wrong?"

He laughed that laugh again, the one that left me breathless.

"No, what I mean is that I like to keep my company professional. I knew you would be good at your job and an asset to the company, but it took anything physical off the table once I hired you. I knew I'd have to sit in my office every day and watch you walking around out there in those dresses and skirts. I would have to watch the way your legs clench together when I'm talking to you and your lips part slightly when we make eye contact and do nothing." He ran his fingers through his hair, but all that did was make me crave to do it to him. "Honestly…" he lifted his drink to his lips, "… it drives me crazy."

Swallowing heavily, it took me three attempts to try speaking before the words came to me. I had asked for his honest answer but somehow wasn't expecting *that* level of openness. His words reflected how I felt, and my stomach twisted in knots as I tried to figure out if that made it better or worse. I liked it when he spoke to me openly and the mask dropped, and then he was exactly the man I knew he was.

On the other hand, his answer had made things so much harder to ignore.

"I think keeping it professional is a good idea."

His expression had shifted into something unreadable where he was just watching me. "You asked."

I nodded slowly. "You're right, I did."

He observed as I continued to run my finger around the glass, a delicate touch circling the rim. I wondered what it would feel like to do the same to the head of his cock.

I cleared my throat, and he looked as though he was about to say something, but before he could speak, I said, "Conference went well today."

"Yes, and I'm sure the next two days will be successful too." He held up his hand as I opened my mouth to answer. "Can we not talk about work? I think we've hurled ourselves past small talk." When I stuttered, he smiled again and pointed to my necklace. "Tell me why you wear that cross. Are you religious?"

I looked down at it, and my hand flinched in response. My instinct had been to touch it, to remind me that it was still there. "No, it was given to me for my fourteenth birthday."

"From your parents?"

"From the priest."

His eyebrows shot up. "A direct gift from a priest? Bit suss."

"Don't be a creep." I slapped him lightly on the shoulder. My heart started racing at the contact, and my breath hitched when I caught his eyes.

I could almost hear his thoughts.

Harder.

"No, it was just a gift. He told me if I wore it, I'd always be protected."

"From what?"

I shrugged. "It's more protected by God, I guess."

"Do you believe in God?"

I raised my eyebrows at him. "Now who's getting into the deep end?" He simply shrugged and waited for an answer but didn't speak. I went back to my glass. "I don't even know anymore. I haven't been to church in a long time, not since boarding school." When I tried to smile, it fell from my lips. "Sometimes, I still talk to God," I mumbled.

"They still have boarding schools?"

"I was sent away. It was basically a convent and very strict."

"Yet you still wear the cross."

"Does it bother you?" I asked, remembering the way he frowned at it during my interview.

"Not at all, just curious to learn more about you."

I nodded.

He didn't know. How could he?

His curiosity had hit on the one thing that I held closest to me—the inciting incident that was the reason for my nightmares, which had been coming back to me in increasing clarity since I moved. The night I hadn't even told Meredith about.

Since being in the city, all those memories had re-formed and painted the image of that night—the night when everything changed. I remembered it now, enough of it to know I didn't want to remember anymore. I feared every night I closed my eyes of the truth that might be revealed to me. Just when I thought I had remembered the worse, more would come back to me. I didn't want it to, I liked not remembering. I had held that secret so close to my chest, it crushed into my heart.

Did my parents remember? Did they know that up until recently, I didn't? They never spoke about it.

The effects of the alcohol swirled through my head. Well, since we were being honest…

Clearing my throat again, I took a sip of the drink Frank had bought after I finished my current one. Hopefully, it would give me the confidence to say what I needed to next.

"Maybe," I started boldly, but my words faded into the sounds of the busy bar with every syllable. "Maybe the protection was from…" I couldn't finish the sentence, but now Frank was looking at me intently, willing the answer from me.

"From?" he prompted as I stared at him, my mouth opening and closing as the words refused to come.

I swallowed. "From the man who attacked me."

Frank started. "Miss Moore, I'm sorry. I didn't

mean to bring up anything troubling."

I waved a hand at him, dismissing his apology. His tone had returned to the professional. He slipped in and out of the role so easily, and I wished I could maintain that level of control around him. I wondered if he did it to protect himself or me. Or both. So far, I had done a reasonable job of maintaining that front. I had exceeded my co-workers' expectations and had managed to keep a relatively professional distance between Frank and me. But when he switched roles so easily, I wondered how honest he really was a moment ago because I certainly couldn't control myself like that around him all of the time.

Barely any of the time, in fact.

Especially now, as he leaned on the bar, sipping at his whiskey, licking those perfect lips of his. Those lips I imagined would be able to find every sensitive spot on my body and exploit them.

If I opened up to him now, the way he had to me, then there would be no going back to the casual friendship we had built and tried to fool ourselves with.

"It's okay." I looked at my feet. "It was a long time ago, although I still have nightmares sometimes." Shaking my head, I still wasn't sure why I was opening up to him. Was it really the alcohol? I hadn't had that much. Or was it just the way I felt so comfortable with him? As though we fit together and had known each other for years. Did I want him to know me, every inch of me, inside and out?

Maybe I wanted him to protect me from the inner demons that haunted me.

Then there was the most pressing question, would I ever find these answers or be forever trying to figure out where I stand with him?

I squeezed my eyes shut for a split second. *Damn, I was in deep.*

"Do you want to tell me what happened?" He leaned forward. We had been joking around since I started, sliding between playful and professional. But this, this was the first time he was truly seeing something of what was beneath the surface. What drove me to be in control, what pushed me to be who I am.

I released a slow breath, followed by a laugh that had no humor behind it. "Wow, this conversation got dark really quick. I'll give you the short version if we can move on after that. Okay?"

"Okay."

"I don't remember it all, I just remember walking home, and I'm not even sure where I was before that. My parents were strict. I wasn't usually allowed out late, but there I was, walking down the street at night. I'm not sure what is memory and what is nightmare at this point, they've been jumbled up in my mind for so long. So, I'm walking, and I'm scared, and I noticed the streetlights are going out, each in succession starting closest to me and working their way down the street. Then I hear whispering, like someone calling me or calling for help. I follow it. Then suddenly, I'm in these woods, I don't know how I got there, and I'm being chased." I tucked my hair behind my ear, looking at my lap again, and felt ridiculous for telling this story. Because that's all it sounded like—a story, a tall tale someone would tell to get attention. Every experience from my teen years had taught me that this story made people stop talking to me or laugh at me.

Or think that I'm crazy.

"When I fall and look up, a man is there, and his eyes… when I look in his eyes, I feel like I'm going to be sick, like just being near him is enough to make my stomach turn. I can't run, I'm so frightened, and he's just looking at me. He's sneering with teeth so sharp I swear he's going to bite me or tear my neck apart, and his eyes, those yellow eyes…"

I was snapped out of my memory at the sound of breaking glass. Looking at Frank, I saw the tumbler had broken in his hand, and the remaining whiskey spilled onto the immaculate bar. He was staring at me, his free hand balled into a shaking fist.

"Frank," I cried, grabbing a napkin from under my drink and prying his fingers apart. There was blood, a lot of blood. "Oh my God, Frank, you need to go to a hospital."

Frank

As we sat at the back of the bar, I listened to her story. She was opening up, and I was finally seeing part of what was inside that head of hers beyond the lust she felt for me, that we felt for each other, and beyond the jokes and casual conversation. I realized I wanted to know every experience that made her and be part of every experience that took her from here to her future.

That last thought staggered me.

For now, it would be easier to pretend I didn't just think that.

But then she reached a part in her story that threw me, and my hand gripped my drink, the glass giving way under my grasp and shattering.

My eyes slowly left her face and fell to my hand. She was frantic and wanted to take me to the hospital.

"No hospital," I grunted. With force, I yanked the pieces of glass from my palm and snatched the dish towel from the bartender as he came over to clean up the mess. Wrapping it around my hand, I stared hard at her, her eyes still on my hands.

"I'm fine."

"At least let me clean you up."

"My room," I grunted. Steadying Charlotte as she jumped unevenly from the bar stool onto her heeled feet, she guided me out of the bar, grabbing my jacket on the way. She kept looking at me like I was going to fall apart, but the blood that drained from my face had nothing to do with the injury to my hand.

No, it was because I recognized her story. I had heard it a hundred times before.

Hell, I had *lived* it just as many times before that, before I left that life behind me.

What she was describing was a demon attack.

CHAPTER
11

Frank

Striding behind the bar of my lavish hotel room, I snatched my jacket from Charlotte and tossed it on the couch, my matching vest twisted with the sharp movements. She was clutching the jacket as though it was a precious commodity, and for some reason, it annoyed me. Perhaps because it was nothing, none of this meant anything, now that I knew what I knew.

"Drink?" I asked her.

"Frank, your hand."

I lifted the dish towel and wiped away the last of the blood, throwing the towel into the bin.

"It's fine. It looked worse than it was. Now, you seem more shaken than I am." I rattled the cocktail shaker. "Drink?"

Charlotte hesitated. "Yes, please."

Mixing up something smooth but strong, I handed Charlotte the glass across the bar before leaning forward on my elbows. The shape of my arms was visible through my shirt's fabric, and I know she noticed. Mike always rolled his eyes at the fitted suits I chose, and he didn't understand why I liked them a bit tight.

That look she gave me, *that* was why.

She stole a glance at my hand as it brushed hers. There were no cuts, no sign of injury. I watched her frown, but I didn't say anything.

What could I say?

I rubbed her arm. Even the slight contact sent a bolt of electricity through me, but I stayed calm. "Are you okay?"

"I'm fine. I am more worried about you."

"Don't be." I watched as she sipped her drink. Rather than finding out more about her, our conversation had resulted only in more questions.

If she had been attacked by a demon when she was a teenager, how far did the attack get? Did it keep her for days? Did it feed on her blood? I wanted to ask and learn *all* the details, even though part of me didn't want to know. But if she remembered, I doubted she'd want to relive it right now. It had been enough for her to open up about what she did remember. I didn't want to re-open that wound.

Not yet.

A nightmare—that's how so many people described the attacks—because after some time, that's all they felt like if they remembered them at all. I had seen a lot of horror movies, and I'm sure that the writers had experienced these attacks and were drawing from their experience, reliving nightmares they didn't even realize were real.

Demons attacked for many reasons—fun, sexual pleasure, or for blood and the sweet life power that it brought, like a drug to us. I watched her neck until I could see the outline of the veins beneath her delicate skin. It had been a long time since I had given into the urge to bring the blood of a human to my lips.

And right now, with her glancing up at me intermittently over her glass, her lipstick stains on the edge as she licked droplets of the liquid from her lips, she looked small and vulnerable. I didn't want her blood. All I wanted to do was pull her close and protect her.

However, the more I visualized pulling her close, the more my head was filled with other distracting ideas. I couldn't be this close to her for more than a few minutes without her calling to me, even if she didn't realize she was doing it. That secret part of her that lay beneath her skin sang to me, and I wanted to claim her.

I *needed* to claim her.

Clearing my throat, I asked, "So, tell me, Miss

Moore, where do you see yourself in five years?"

"Charlotte," she whispered.

"Charlotte," I repeated, letting the suave ooze from my voice until she'd realize her name had never sounded better than when I said it. "Same question."

"This is sounding very much like an interview question. Are you trying to distract me?"

My laugh was sudden and loud, followed by, "I have better ways to distract you." This caused her cheeks to flame. Why was she embarrassed around me? She had already revealed her biggest secret to me, but maybe that was it. Maybe she had opened the door to her vulnerability and was now desperate to close it again.

Before it was too late.

It was already too late.

"Sorry." I lifted a shoulder. "I guess I'm not very good at flirting." I couldn't help but grin.

Such a lie.

Charlotte raised her eyebrow. "That's an absolute lie, so it must be a line in itself."

My smile turned wicked. "You got me."

All walls were down now. This back and forth had built up inside of me, and I couldn't take it anymore. I came around from behind the bar and closed the space between us. I could drop the mask as quickly and efficiently as I could put it on. Professional Frank. Playful Frank. Flirty Frank.

But this was different.

This made things harder because I was *allowing* her to see all sides of me.

For every step I took, there was a part of me telling me to stop and step back because every inch I got closer to her made me lose control of my resolve a little bit more.

Charlotte didn't move. I could almost see her mind fighting with her body.

The way she bit her lip told me her mind was racing. I was her *boss*. She agreed to come to my hotel room with me. Did she really think this was about treating an injury? Or having a drink? She knew what this was.

Did I?

She was so achingly close, and she wasn't moving away.

I could smell her perfume, a subtle floral scent, and if I breathed in deep enough, I could smell her skin beneath the artificial scent. My legs almost buckled.

She was wet.

We were alone, and all the possibilities of the things we could do ran through my mind. We had all night, uninterrupted. We could pretend that beyond these walls, the world outside didn't exist. We could pretend there were no consequences. She could push the worries about her job aside and just let herself go.

She was so close to me, the brush of my shirt fabric tingled against her exposed arms, her hand twitched, and the other clenched around her glass.

She was resisting.

She swallowed, whispering, "Is that what this is, real flirting?"

My voice intoxicated her, and I let it. I shouldn't, but it was hard not to. Seduction was a part of me, and I couldn't turn it off, not when she was this close. "Isn't it?"

Brushing my fingers down her arm, she shivered under my touch. There it was again—the need to protect, to possess, to make her mine. The idea that another demon had touched her only surged me on. She was no one's to touch but mine—not human or demon. She was mine and mine alone. I wanted to touch her, to take her, to make her cry my name over and over and bring her to the peak of pleasure before letting her have a release when I, and only I, said she could.

"Well, since you're on to all my games, maybe we can try something else..." I whispered.

Charlotte trembled as I took her glass and placed it on the bar with mine. She never stopped looking at my face with those beautiful eyes, wide and innocent, like she didn't know what was going to happen.

She knew.

Part of me reminded me this was wrong, that I

shouldn't act on this, that I should have more control. But all the tensions which had been swirling around inside me had come to the surface, threatening to burst forth and take control.

And Charlotte, well, she could barely breathe, let alone find any willpower within herself to say *stop*.

Because she didn't want me to.

I knew it.

Using my fingertips, I brushed her arm again, eliciting a gasp from Charlotte. Her hands shook with the effort not to touch me back, but she was fighting a losing battle. This was more than physical attraction, it was animal. I'd both protect and own her, and by giving herself completely to me, she'd still be in control.

Sort of.

"Frank..."

"Yes?"

She only gasped again as I placed a hand on her cheek and leaned down, her sharp intake of breath felt against my lips, so close to hers but not quite touching. She made a sound somewhere between a moan and a whimper. My breathing was ragged.

This was torture for me to move so slowly.

But it was so much fun torturing her.

"I don't think this is a good idea," she whispered against my lips.

"Nothing fun ever is," I whispered back, my voice still deep and dark, the best kind of intoxication sweeping over her trembling body. "Tell me you don't want this. Tell me you don't want me inside you."

"I can't." Charlotte shook her head even as her hands trailed up my stomach and chest, coming down to fiddle with the buttons on my shirt. "We shouldn't," she whispered as she popped one of the buttons open. She stared at it as though that button represented all the control she had left to stop herself.

As her hands moved down I watched her face, while she flicked open the obstacles the buttons posed one at a time. "Then stop," I growled.

It was a dare. Because if she didn't, I certainly wouldn't.

"I can't..."

Lowering my face to hers again, Charlotte parted her lips as I moved closer and slowly ran my hand up her waist and over the underside of her breast. I had one arm poised on thc wall next to her head, my muscles tensed with the effort of taking it slowly, savoring the smell and feel of her.

My lips brushed hers, those perfect lips I longed to hear moan. I wanted to make her say my name, to take her, make her mine, to possess her.

Pressing my lips to hers, she gasped against the kiss, and just as she moved to part her lips...

The phone rang.

"Shit." I dropped my head, the rage bubbling in

my chest, and I only moved when the phone persisted in its interruption in what I was sure was about to be the moment she gave herself to me. Letting my hand fall from her body, I gruffly took the phone from my pocket.

"What?" I barked. I listened for a moment and watched Charlotte as she subconsciously crossed her arms over her chest and rubbed her upper arms.

I'd already lost her.

I could see it in her eyes.

She was in her head again, thinking too much.

"Okay, give me five," I mumbled.

I threw the phone to the bed, resuming my position in front of her with one hand pressed against the wall, my chest pressed against hers, and my lips near her ear.

"I'm sorry, I have an emergency phone meeting to attend," I whispered, trailing my lips across her earlobe, nibbling at her sensitive skin.

Charlotte shuddered, closing her eyes and getting lost in the feel of it.

For a moment.

She stepped out from under my arm, straightening her clothes. "It's probably for the best." She looked at the floor, whispering, "This is very unprofessional."

Who was she trying to convince?

I simply watched her, my muscles straining in

my shirt against the temptation to tie her to the bed and make her wait until I was done with the phone call.

I was so close to having her.

"You can wait here," I offered, but the words sounded more like a command. Throwing a glance at the bed, Charlotte pressed her lips together, and I growled deep in my throat when I sensed the rush between her legs.

She was tempted.

But she took the smallest step backward, and when I didn't say anything, she raised her eyes to mine. When her eyes widened, I cursed myself. I knew what she had seen. For just a moment, for a split second, I had lost control of my demon, and the yellow had flashed across my eyes. But she shook her head, and when I tilted my chin up, she continued to look into my eyes.

After a beat, I simply said, "Okay." Because what else could I say?

Her lips were still pressed together, and I hoped she could taste me on them, and that it tortured her. The way her eyes pleaded with me, I could see that she was hoping I wasn't angry or upset. But she could also see the darkness clouding my expression, and I made sure my eyes promised her that this wasn't over.

She wouldn't be able to resist me forever.

I knew she didn't want to resist forever.

Charlotte moved toward the door to leave the hotel room, her hand shaking as she took the cold door handle in her fingers. "Good night, Mr. Blackman."

A muscle ticked in my jaw. "Good night, Miss Moore."

Charlotte

He had backed off, and I couldn't pretend it didn't hurt.

After all, I had turned him down. The phone call had broken the trance, and I had been snapped back to reality in the harshest way. I could've stayed in the room, waited for the call to finish, and let him come back to me on the bed and touch me again. This time there would be no interruptions, nothing to break the spell of how good he felt. A spike of desire grew in my abdomen at the thought. But when he answered that call, all I saw was my boss, and the absolute realization of how the next step could've been the biggest mistake I could make for my career slapped me in the face, full force, and once again, the indecision took over, making me a shuddering mess.

The biggest mistake or the best night of my life.

Or both.

At the same time I had opened up to him, we had

opened up to each other. We had been completely honest about our desires and demons and had let our individual walls down, if only for a few hours. My choice to step away hadn't been easy, and I wanted to tell him that. I wanted to make sure he knew how much it cut me inside to take that first step away from him because it was almost physically painful to do so.

I kept trying to tell myself I did the right thing.

But the way his face had darkened had knocked the breath from me, and I couldn't explain, could barely speak.

The rest of the conference had been uneventful, the following evening's dinner with clients had been full of false laughs and comradery. Frank had made some good connections, but he was distracted. His fingers drummed absentmindedly on his thigh as he talked. I had noticed the way Frank appeared to snarl when one of the potential clients tried to pick me up, offering me a drink in his room. Obviously, I turned him down, but I had not been able to meet Frank's eyes for the rest of the night, as though I was already guilty. Feeling his gaze as it followed me around the room, he'd resolutely look away whenever I built up the courage to return the stare.

After a notably silent flight home, where a word was barely spoken between us and he'd ignored me when I'd offered him a drink, his only response being a twitch that jumped in his jaw, I felt myself growing angry.

Why *should* I feel bad? I was the one doing the right thing and maintaining a professional distance when he had crossed that line. Or had I crossed it when I opened up to him at the bar? Shaking my head to myself, my brow knitted together, and my lips pressed into a thin line. It didn't matter who had made the first move, I had done the right thing in shutting it down, and I had done nothing since but try to continue communicating with him. He had shut me down in harsher ways than I ever did him.

The following day we were back at the office, and I was sure others had noticed the change in his behavior toward me, but no one said anything, of which I was glad. I didn't feel there was any suitable way to explain to my co-workers what had changed at the conference. I knew that eventually, I'd have to move on professionally if I were to achieve my dream and climb through the industry, and I didn't want whatever this was to ruin my integrity or reputation. If potential future employers thought I had slept my way up the ladder, my career was over before it started.

I had entertained the thought of perhaps pursuing something with Frank when I moved on with my career, but that was before he started acting like a petulant child at being turned down.

As the days drew on, if ever I were alone with Frank, there would be moments when he'd laugh. Not the same laughter as before, but still a genuine chuckle, even if the sound broke off too soon. It wouldn't take long before his smirk would drop, and he'd look at me, the warmth draining from his eyes and being replaced with that darkness that should scare me but didn't. The mask would return, and he would be the same man I had first met. A man with power who knew how to use it and always got what he wanted. A man who didn't take well to having what he wanted taken from him.

If I were honest with myself, it was still what I wanted too.

I had all these reasons and points I could remind myself of when I was debating inside my mind. All these things I could run over to convince myself I did the right thing.

All these things.

So, why did it feel so wrong to have turned him away?

CHAPTER 12

Frank

Every day for the following week, I watched as Charlotte came into the office. Slightly early, as always, and cradling a coffee in one hand with her oversized handbag dangling from her other arm. As she dropped her sunglasses and phone on the desk, her lips would part as she released a sigh. I knew why she was sighing, the effort of trying to put things back how they were between us was draining, but she couldn't shove it all back in the box now. It was out.

That, and I wouldn't let her put it back to how it was.

We had admitted to each other there was something beyond an attraction between us, and I wouldn't go back now.

I couldn't.

Charlotte had gotten underneath my skin, and now I thought I had an inkling as to why. The knowledge another demon had touched her made me territorial, and I had to grit my teeth to contain the red and black markings that were threatening to surface beneath my skin when I thought about it. It didn't make complete sense as the attack had seemed fairly run-of-the-mill.

But there was something else.

"Good morning, Mr. Blackman," she called through my open door, that smile plastered on her face that didn't quite travel to her eyes.

I didn't respond because I didn't trust myself.

Since the end of the conference, I had been swinging wildly between contradicting emotions—anger, hurt, possessiveness, resignation, anger, and possessiveness again. While I understood her reasons for turning me down, there were a few things wrong with the scenario when I played it out in my head as I lay in bed, staring angrily at the ceiling.

Some nights I'd imagine that the night at the conference had played out differently, and fist my cock under the sheets, thinking of her mouth on me.

Firstly, women didn't turn me down. Period. I never forced, not once, but charm was second nature to me, and women responded to that. Secondly, I was *so sure* she was about to give herself to me that night. I could feel it radiating from her, a powerful heat that almost knocked the air from my lungs. The need to come apart and be taken, not just by anyone, but specifically by me. My cock twitched in my pants, and I adjusted in my chair, glancing up to see if she was watching me.

She wasn't.

If my phone hadn't rung, if I didn't have to put my business first, within half an hour, she'd have been writhing under me as I pounded into her, and I clasped a hand over her mouth to muffle her moans from traveling through the thin hotel walls.

I had thrown the occasional flirtatious line at her, and she had laughed in return. On the surface, it was like we had gone back to how we were before.

Mostly.

It was increasingly difficult to maintain the charade, though, and my fingers would twitch when she was close, aching to touch her. She'd smile, but her eyes told a different story, and I couldn't tell if the regret I saw was for what happened or what didn't. So, I kept closed off to her, not knowing if I'd eventually give in first or she would.

It was another week before I started losing control,

forced to bring myself off every morning before work, imagining her doing the same in her bed while thinking of me. I didn't want to seek the company of other women, although I could have. No one else but her would do to quench this thirst. The small release was barely enough to get me through each day.

That morning Charlotte brought me the reports from the previous week, perfectly on time, as always.

"Good morning, Miss Moore."

"Morning, Mr. Blackman. Reports for you."

As Charlotte placed them on the desk in front of me, she watched as my eyes lingered on her breasts before reaching her face. She pushed her shoulders back to enunciate her curves, and the corner of her lip twitched when my eyes widened. I stared at her—she was playing games with me now.

Right.

"Did you have a good weekend?" I asked after a lazy pause. It was the first time I had started a conversation with her in several days, and if she was trying to hide her surprise, she failed.

"Yes, I did. I finished moving into my new apartment."

"Lovely, maybe you can show it to me sometime."

Charlotte just looked at me after a beat, returning my grin. "Maybe," was all she offered. I could tell the friendliness of the expression wasn't real. I knew the way her lips framed her teeth when she really smiled, and it wasn't the thin-lipped curve she was presenting to me now.

I couldn't take any more of this shit. I'd never been hung up on any one woman before, and this needed to end.

Now.

As she turned to leave, I stood and grabbed her arm, spinning her around to face me. Automatically, she glanced out the glass doors, but no one was passing to see how I was holding her, arms around her waist and chest to chest.

I stared into her eyes, piercing her with my gaze, and growled, "How long are we going to pretend that nothing happened?"

"As long as it takes."

"Until?"

"Until we can find a way to work together again," she muttered.

"Is that really what you want?"

Charlotte looked down, biting her lip against the truth that threatened to burst forth from her. Because I knew the truth, I saw the slightest shake of her head, not sure if she was even aware her body had betrayed her. It was the only confirmation I needed. I didn't want to play games any longer. I'd either have her, or I wouldn't. If the answer was no, she needed to tell me because otherwise, I wasn't going to stop.

Not until I got what I wanted.

There was something about her, something she wasn't showing me, and until I figured out what it was, I couldn't get it out of my mind. The way she reacted when we touched just about had me taking her right then and there in the office, sweeping my desk clear and bending her over it.

Who cares who saw? I wanted everyone to know the claim I had. That I owned Charlotte.

"Let me take you out to dinner."

Charlotte arched an eyebrow at me—the comment surprised me as much as it did her.

Dinner? I didn't *do* dinner. I did drinks and then sex, coffee, then sex, sex, and then more sex. Not dinner dates, not dates at all. Charlotte watched my face, trying to figure out if this was simply another flirtatious comment with no real intent behind it or a genuine offer.

"Strictly professional?"

"Of course." I grinned. We both knew it was a lie. "To congratulate you on all your hard work."

"What time?"

"Seven."

"I'll need to get the subway home then meet you—"

"I'll take you home, so you can get changed."

Her eyebrow was still arched, and she pulled away from me. Relinquishing my hold on her immediately, I did it only because I was satisfied knowing it wouldn't be the last time I held her. She paused, looking at me, weighing her options.

Charlotte bit her bottom lip, apparently fighting a battle inside her body and mind. I suspected there was still that voice telling her that this was a bad idea, that having me in her home would be a mistake.

Because if we were alone with no distractions, I wouldn't be able to stop myself.

To feel what was beneath her clothes, under my fingers, my tongue…

Soon.

She watched me for a beat longer before nodding stiffly and turning to leave. "Will that be all, Mr. Blackman?"

"That'll be all."

My words were professional, but my sneer was full of promise.

I know she noticed.

My hesitations were few. As far as I was concerned, we had already crossed the line and might as well go all the way now. Once she invited me into her home, that would be it, and I'd have no control left. I could stand at that doorway forever and wait, knowing I could cross the threshold and have her, but the invitation excited me.

Because she had no idea what she was in for when she unleashed the demon in me.

Alone in my office, the corners of my lips curled into a snarl.

The day went slowly, and finally the time had come where I practically ushered her out the door and into my car. I didn't trust myself to talk during the drive. I could see her glancing at me in my peripheral vision. She'd open her mouth to say something, then close it again. I knew how she felt. I was teetering on the edge of control myself—everything pent up inside me at the prospect of finally getting her underneath me.

At this point, I didn't care what Mike would say.

There was no going back now.

Charlotte

We drove in silence. I had given Frank my address, and he had needed no further direction, knowing the area better than I did. Settling down in the leather seat, the car was spacious and screamed luxury and wealth. Something I was not yet familiar with.

I became nervous about him seeing my apartment. It was classy and open-spaced, at least I thought so, and it was certainly much more lavish than anywhere I had lived previously. But it was still sparsely furnished with boxes around the place. I didn't have much to bring with me and hadn't yet purchased all the furniture I needed.

The coffee table *was* a box, for God's sake.

Frank looked over at me, both of his hands tense on the steering wheel. I know my nerves were radiating from me, and his eyes kept flickering down to my cleavage and over my legs, and he'd grip the steering wheel harder each time.

He parked hastily in my assigned guest parking spot and exited the car, slamming the door behind him a bit too hard before opening mine. I stepped out of the car on shaky legs and led him to the elevator.

Stepping out of the elevator, I tried not to think about how Frank's eyes would be following my movements as we walked down the narrow hall to my new apartment. The apartment that I was only able to put a deposit on because of my new job.

I must remember to thank him for the opportunity.

I had a feeling I was about to.

"I'll only need a minute to get changed. You know you didn't need to walk me to my door."

Frank hummed his acknowledgment but didn't say anything further.

The hum bordered on a growl, and my skin tingled.

My rules about relationships with co-workers were rapidly deteriorating around me, and I could feel it melting with my resolve. I had no inclination to stop it.

The way we looked at each other every time I brought a file into his office was too much, and now it had built up into this, ready to explode at the slightest provocation. Frank looked as though he was going to devour me on the spot as I stood by his desk some days, and God knows I wouldn't have protested if he had laid me out on his desk earlier today.

He was right behind me as I fumbled with my keys, so achingly close.

Oh God, having him in my apartment was a terrible idea.

CHAPTER 13

Charlotte

"Nice building," he said simply as we stood outside my apartment door, his voice tight.

"Guess I should say thank you." I unlocked the door, dropping my handbag and jacket on the floor and kicking off my heels, glad to be rid of them. I looked back, and Frank was watching me. His gaze trailed up from my feet to my eyes, dropping to my chest again as I rubbed my neck, feeling exposed at his wandering gaze.

He was standing at the threshold.

Why wasn't he coming in?

"Please." I held my arm out. "Come in."

He advanced with long, confident strides, closing the gap between us in a handful and kicking the door closed behind him, his look daring me to protest at the loud slam.

When I was backed against the wall, his body pressed against mine, he punched his knuckles into the plaster on either side of my head, and I yelped. He hadn't damaged anything, but I had seen what he could do. So he must be controlling himself with whatever little control he had left.

I held my breath.

There was no going back now.

"Would you like a tour?" I asked, breathless.

"Does the tour end in the bedroom?" he growled.

A sharp gasp escaped my lips. He was so close to me I could feel the heat of his body through our clothes.

Too many clothes.

"*Yes.*"

Frank nodded stiffly, the muscles in his arms visibly tensing through his shirt as he strained to stay still. "Let's cut right to the end then."

Nodding, I ducked out from under his arm and we moved toward the bedroom. He followed close behind me, and the moment I crossed the threshold, he was on me. Pushing me against the wall, his mouth was hot and needy against mine. I mumbled a series of nonsensical sounds as he moved down, licking and nipping at my neck while he undid my dress.

Fast, practiced movements had my head spinning.

"Frank," I gasped, placing a hand on his chest as

he shrugged his jacket off, fighting with the sleeves as they threatened to hold him back from touching me before throwing it to the side.

"What?" He had unzipped my dress and moved his hands to my shoulders, seconds from pulling it off and exposing me to him.

"We can't let this affect our professional relationship," I whispered.

Who was I kidding? But part of me just kept reminding me how hard I had worked to be where I am, and I didn't want to throw that away for one night.

However good that night might be.

"Of course," he mumbled. I wasn't sure if he was really listening, but it was all I needed right now. Later, I could tell myself that I had made some effort and had tried to put back the boundaries that had already been so ruthlessly demolished.

As my dress fell to the floor, I stepped out of it, only to be pushed back against the wall by Frank's body.

"Are you done talking now?" he growled, and I nodded as I squeezed my hands between our bodies and started unbuttoning his shirt. "Good," he said as he grabbed my chin, tilting my head up to look at him, my fingers stalled in their ministrations, and he snarled. "Because the next word you say better be my name." He grunted and leaned back enough to undo the top button and yank his shirt over his head, not prepared to wait for my hands to stop stumbling over the buttons. He returned his attention to my neck and collarbone, now slightly red, either from the blood rushing to my face or the irritation from his stubble.

Or both.

As he sunk his teeth into my shoulder, I gasped again.

He was marking me.

Frank pressed his lips to mine, pushing my mouth open with his tongue as I gave in to his touch. His lips were soft, gentle, warming me up from the inside out with expert maneuvers. As he explored my mouth with his tongue, I moaned, imagining that tongue working its way around other areas of my body. When he started massaging my breasts through my bra, I gasped again.

What was wrong with me? One touch from this man, and I fell apart. I wanted to take some control in the bedroom, to unleash the part of me that I had so recently discovered.

But when Frank touched me, all I could concentrate on was the tingle of my skin under his mouth and fingers and the growing warmth between my thighs. I melted against him, completely lost within the feel of him and with no desire to fight any longer.

I didn't want him to think I was the type to just go limp in his arms and have him do all the work, but I was liquescent against him, barely having the strength to stand on my own.

"You're wearing too many clothes," he mumbled against my skin, unhooking my bra with one hand and tugging at my panties with the other. I ground my hips against his hand as he grazed the front of my underwear.

"You can talk." I chuckled, fumbling with the belt and fly on his pants.

Frank pulled back out of my grasp and grabbed my breasts, rubbing them gently as his teeth grazed down my neck, leaving another mark on me as he nipped at my skin.

I was his.

Even if the marks he left would be hidden beneath my clothes, we'd both know they were there. Every time he'd see me in the office, he would know. Every time I would get changed in front of a mirror I'd remember that he claimed me—he owned me.

He worked his way down my body, kissing in between my breasts and over my stomach. Linking his fingers in my panties, Frank pulled them down, leaving them in a pile at my feet while he took me in with his eyes.

"Well, aren't you a pretty little thing?" He hummed as he kissed my stomach, making me moan softly. "Even more so without those little dresses you wear around the office teasing me, enticing me…"

"I was just—" But what I was *just…* Frank never found out because my words were cut off with another gasp as his lips found my hip bone. I grabbed at his hair, pulling him to me.

"Eager, aren't we?" Frank chuckled. "So worried about our work relationship yet coming undone the moment I…" He licked between my legs quickly, barely touching me, but it was enough to entice another moan from my lips.

I squeezed my eyes shut for a moment, seemingly to have lost the ability to talk.

Everywhere he touched me was sensory overload, and I wanted more, yet he seemed intent on teasing me. After the night at the conference, I thought he'd ravage me given a second chance. But every move of my hips toward his mouth made him chuckle and pull back, only teasing me more. His hands held me still against the wall, clamping on my thighs with unbridled strength.

Another mark, I'm sure.

My eyes snapped open as, ever so gently, he slid his tongue between my pussy lips and then, just as slowly, over my clit, flicking his tongue over my bud.

"Oh *God!*"

He pulled back. "Call me Frank…" he bared his teeth, "… or if you fancy being dirty, you can call me Mr. Blackman."

I chuckled. "You're not the boss of me."

Frank responded by another lick over my clit, making me jump. "I am. I am your boss out of the bedroom, and now…" he licked me again, "… I'm the boss in here too."

I managed a shaky nod and grabbed his shoulders, gripping with my fingertips.

"Just please…" I moaned, "… don't stop."

He was on his feet, pressing me against the wall again, knocking the air from my lungs with the force of being slammed against the plasterboard. His fingers ran through my hair, making me moan, the moan breaking off when he tangled his fingers and yanked my head back.

"What was that you said?"

I stuttered. The contrast between his gentle attention a moment before and the rough dominance now caught me off guard. "I… I just—"

"Were you…" he licked his lips, "… begging me?"

I nodded, then stopped when each nod made my hair pull on my scalp as he tightened his grip.

"Do it again," he whispered against my neck. "Beg me."

"What?"

"You heard me." He twisted my hair around his hand again, bringing his fist up to my scalp. "Beg."

"Please, touch me."

He tugged my hair back again, exposing my neck to him as I arched, and he ran his tongue up my collarbone to my cheek.

"You can do better than that. Do you want me to touch you? To lick you?"

I whimpered.

How was I supposed to find the words?

When he was…

Just. So. Close.

"Do you want me to fuck you hard? Slow? Do you want me to tease you?"

He started teasing my body with his fingers, barely touching me, a featherlight touch that made me shiver. I was about to tell him where he could shove his featherlight touch when he pinched my nipple between his fingers, bringing another gasp to my lips.

"Do you touch yourself when you think of me?" he whispered. When I nodded, pushing my chest against his touch, he growled, "Dirty girl."

Every word tumbling from his lips was ecstasy. I was so ready for him, but he was making me wait, perhaps payback for when I turned him down. Maybe he was into torture. Maybe he liked watching the way I squirmed, trying desperately to get him to touch me with the sporadic movement of my hips. I glanced down, straining because I couldn't move far from his vice-like grip on my hair. He was so hard, I could see the outline of him through his pants, but apparently, he was having too much fun with me.

So I gave in.

"Please, please, Frank," I begged, gyrating my hips, desperate for the friction he was denying me. "Please touch me, take me, own me. Please *fuck me.* Frank…"

"That's what I wanted to hear." He released my hair and kneeled in front of me again. He ran his tongue up my pussy, a single lick over my clit, and I jumped in reaction, already sensitive to his touch and emitting a small, "Oh!"

He did it again and again. I wanted desperately to spread my legs and give him full access, but he held my thighs together, making me wait and teasing me.

He kept going until I was close and had me teetering on the edge of release. I was trembling, leaning against the wall, my legs barely able to hold me up.

My breaths became rapid. "Frank, please." I gasped. "Please, make me come."

Pulling away, he chuckled as I whimpered, "Oh no, not yet." Giving me one final lick, he whispered, "Not yet," I groaned loudly in frustration as he pulled away, his breath hot against my mound.

As Frank stood, I could feel his erection through his pants against my stomach as he pressed his body against mine, his naked torso rubbing against my already sensitive nipples. I grasped at his shoulders, trying to pull him closer, desperate for the release he had denied me. But the jerk just grinned.

Kissing me hard, I relinquished to his dominance. I recoiled slightly as I tasted myself, but as I ran my hands over his shoulders and feeling his muscles tense and release beneath my fingers, I leaned into him. Frank trapped me between him and the wall, every inch of his skin against mine was ecstasy. He radiated heat.

Hooking one arm under my knees, he lifted me, his mouth attached to my neck in a series of playful nips and bites as I wrapped my arms around his shoulders. Carrying me to the bed, he then tossed me down onto the mattress.

I watched, breathless, as he finished undressing. My eyes wandered hungrily over his naked body as he stood at the edge of the bed, watching me like a predator would watch prey. This time I welcomed the look, the anticipation crawling across my skin.

His smile was dangerous as he beckoned me to the edge of the bed.

"Taste it," he said, taking his erection in his hand and rubbing himself.

Crawling toward the edge of the bed, I opened my mouth eagerly, and Frank placed one hand on the back of my head and eased his cock between my waiting lips. He moaned slowly as I moved him in and out of my mouth, looking up at him through my lashes.

My jaw ached after a while, but I didn't care.

I wanted to submit to him, and I wanted to take control.

I wanted it all.

As long as it was with him.

Behind his expression emanated danger and menace that darkened with every stroke of him I made, every dip of my tongue down to the base of his cock. I didn't feel unsafe, but the element of lurking danger behind his eyes made my body flush with arousal. I could feel his control teetering and knew I was playing a dangerous game by teasing him the way he teased me. But I wanted the animal I knew lurked underneath, the one I had seen crouching behind his eyes as he watched me in the office.

I welcomed it, demanded it.

Wrapping his hands around my hair again, he pulled it into a ponytail and took control, guiding my head as he thrust into my mouth.

I let him.

He built up speed, a few quick thrusts before pulling out and leaning in to kiss me again, sucking on my tongue, turning it dirty. He did it again, pushing his full length into my mouth, ignoring the slight gag, and holding me still. When I squirmed, he'd pull almost all the way out, just enough to allow me to gasp for breath before pushing it back in. When I gripped my fingernails into his thigh, he pulled out, a devilish grin playing on his lips as I coughed.

I looked up at him, and for a moment, I thought I saw concern in his eyes as though he was worried about how I'd react to his treatment of me. But my gaze was blurred and my eyelids heavy with arousal.

I loved it.

Now he knew I liked him taking control, I could tell by his smug expression, and I wanted him to do it. It was permission for him to break that next level of control he was holding on to. I could feel it around him in the way he still slightly tremored when he touched me. Even though his touch was rough, he was still holding on to control. Using my hair to tilt my face up to his, he bent down and growled against my swollen lips, "Tell me you want me."

"I want you, Frank, please."

"Do you want me to take you? Dominate you?"

My eyes fluttered closed at his words until he tugged on my hair, waiting for me to lock eyes with him. "Tell me," he hissed. "I want to hear you beg for my cock."

"Please, please." My words came out in a tumbled rush, every inch of my skin was on fire with the prospect of him touching me, and I was desperate for more of him. "Frank, please take me. I can't stand it."

Pushing me back onto the bed roughly, Frank crawled over my naked body as I scooted toward the headboard. Lying in between the pillows, I marveled at his body as he braced himself above me, and I wanted to memorize every line of his muscles, his arms, his chest—everything. The hunger in his eyes fueled mine and filled me. I could almost see his muscles ripping underneath his skin. I watched his arms tense, unable to tear my eyes from him as he braced himself on either side of my head. Aching for the feel of him on top of me, I moaned as his large body pinned mine to the bed.

I couldn't help it, the vocalizing. It was drawn from me, every whimper and moan.

And I didn't care because the sounds were drawn by him.

"Frank," I whispered, gazing into his eyes and running my hands over every inch of his body I could reach. I was saying everything without saying it, and I didn't think I had any words left.

Take me.

I whispered his name again and gasped as his hand traveled down my body and slapped gently at the inside of my thighs, spreading my legs apart when I didn't move fast enough. His breathing was ragged. He was losing control.

Good.

Frank leaned forward and practically growled against my skin. "Give yourself to me."

My eyes glazed over as he guided his cock inside me, slowly at first. I assumed he was allowing me time to become accustomed to his girth, and I was grateful. His grin was smug right before I squeezed my eyes shut.

Fuck.

"Need a moment?" The pride was evident in his voice, and I'd have chastised him if it weren't for the distracting protest of my body. He moaned loudly, the sound dominating the room as I clenched around him. Frank stopped moving when I spread my legs for him, my fingers gripping his shoulders as I eased myself into the delectable stretch of him. I couldn't spread my legs any further, but lord knows I tried to ease the pressure. It was like my first time all over again, and every inch in my body screamed at me that I couldn't take any more. But this was different because I wanted *more*. My eyes snapped open when a shift from him resulted in a spark of pleasure on my clit.

The smug bastard had found the right angle, and he *knew it*.

Smiling against my neck, he leaned forward. "You ready?"

He didn't wait for an answer before pulling almost all the way out and then pounding back into me in one movement.

Hard.

I cried out with every thrust, each moan louder as he built speed. I started gasping with each thrust, completely under his spell and unable to break eye contact with him. He held my gaze as his arms on either side of my head tensed before he cushioned the top of my head with his palms while he thrust harder, deeper, relishing in every tiny sound that escaped my lips as I bent my legs back, giving him access to all of me.

A position I'd have been embarrassed about with anyone else.

But not him.

"Oh fuck, *yes*," he groaned, and I tightened around him with the change of angle. When I cried out again, he clamped a hand over my mouth, and my eyes widened. "Shh, pet. Let me fuck you." I moaned against his hand, writhing beneath him as he arched into the feel of my nails gripping his back. I worried I was gripping too hard, but then I saw the ecstasy on his face and did it harder.

The muscles in his right arm tensed as he shifted his weight, using his left hand to trail down my body, slowly teasing my skin with his fingertips, pinching my nipples before moving down further. When he found my clit with his fingers and started rubbing in small tight circles, I gasped and gripped his shoulders. His smile was arrogant as he continued to thrust into me, finding a perfect rhythm with his hand and bringing me a pleasure no one had managed before.

Not even me.

"Oh!" I cried out. "Oh my—"

"Oh my *what,* pet?"

"Oh, oh." I could barely breathe, let alone pull together an articulated thought or sentence. I spread my legs wider for him, wanting to take every inch of him inside me, aching for release.

He pressed harder with his fingers.

"Frank!" As my peak hit and I screamed his name, he continued to work my clit, forcing me to ride out the waves of pleasure. I came apart beneath him and felt my warmth flush around his cock. My hips bucked against his hand as he maintained a steady pressure until I was whimpering at his assault of my already sensitive body.

"Mmm..." he hummed, licking his fingers before holding them in front of my lips. "Suck," he commanded.

Degrading.

So fucking hot.

Without hesitation, I opened my mouth and sucked his fingers, tasting my arousal on his skin. He groaned as he watched me, never letting me drop eye contact with him as I worked my tongue around his fingers. I felt a flicker of guilt at allowing myself to submit to this man, my *boss*, and crossing that line between professional and personal that I told myself I never would. But as I twitched with every residual touch on my clit, and with his every movement, I forgot myself.

Something was burning beneath my skin, something clawing to get out.

Something I could release with him.

Watching my eyelids flutter in my post-orgasmic bliss, he removed his fingers from my mouth before tracing them along my lips and down my neck. He had slowed his thrusts to a gentle, steady rhythm while my breathing returned to normal.

His voice turned dark as he leaned in close to my face. "My turn."

The sound that escaped my lips, a peep of sorts, was embarrassing. But he just kept that smug grin on his face as he dropped himself to his elbows and thrust into me once, harder than before. I cried out and grabbed his shoulders once more, hissing praises through my teeth.

"Again," I cried.

Frank complied and did it just once more before building up his speed until the bed was rocking with the power of his thrusts. I couldn't speak, only managing to make soft moans as he continued to fuck me, bringing himself toward his peak.

Using me.

Please use me, always.

"Oh, fuck, you are…. So. Damn. Tight," he moaned, punctuating each word with another thrust. "I could fuck you all night." He leaned toward my face, taking my bottom lip in his teeth briefly. "Maybe I will. Maybe I'll fuck that pussy until it's raw, and you're begging for mercy. Maybe I'll keep you locked up and use you as I please."

A tremble ran through my body at his words, at the drunk, ecstatic quality his voice had taken on. I was lost in him as he moved within me.

"You're on birth control, right?" He panted, sweat glistening on his forehead. I didn't answer, I couldn't. I just nodded hastily and pulled him against me.

Reaching down again, he hooked my leg over his shoulder, running his hand between my thighs again, and flicked his fingers over my sensitive clit.

"Oh no, Frank, I can't, I can't." I panted.

"I want you to come with me."

"I can't—"

"I want to feel you orgasm around my cock."

"*Frank.*" He rubbed harder, forcing me to another orgasm.

I cried out, and my back arched off the bed as I came again, bunching the sheets beneath my desperate fingers. Frank grabbed my hips and tilted me toward him as he thrust deep, roaring as he came inside me. He continued rocking against me until we were both panting before collapsing on top of me.

Frank breathed heavily against my neck while I stroked his back, memorizing the shape of his muscles with my fingertips. I could feel his lips against the crook of my neck and shoulder, a smile playing on his mouth.

Damn him, the smug bastard was so proud of himself.

My leg twitched.

Damn him again, because he had every right to be proud.

After a short while, I felt his weight shift as he dropped onto me further and became heavy.

"Frank?" When he didn't respond, I shook his shoulders gently. "Frank?"

He jolted, then mumbled against my skin, his breath warm. "Call me, Mr. Blackman." I chuckled as he braced himself up on one arm and looked down at me. "Sorry, don't usually do that." He frowned. "The way you were touching me was so relaxing..." He let his voice trail off.

But then, the moment was gone, and he grinned again, sitting up and swinging one leg over the edge of the bed. I sat up, pulling the sheet with me. "Are you leaving?"

"Just getting a water..." He paused. "Unless you want me to leave?"

"No."

He arched his eyebrow at my hasty response, and I looked at him earnestly. I didn't care that I had answered too quickly. The entire experience had been unbelievable, incredibly intense and had left me feeling vulnerable. When he didn't speak, and the silence stretched out between us, I became uncomfortable.

"I mean if you want to leave…" I added quietly.

Frank turned around slightly and leaned forward until his lips were a hair's breadth away from mine. "Charlotte…" he whispered, pulling the sheet from my grip and running his hand over my exposed breast. Goosebumps formed on my skin following his touch. "Are you asking me for round two?"

I opened and closed my mouth a few times without speaking.

Yes.

"Oooh, you do want more," he crooned, abandoning his mission to get a drink and crawling over me.

I placed a palm on his chest. "Actually, a drink sounds good. I need to catch my breath, and I think you promised me dinner?"

"Does that mean you have to put clothes on?"

"We could order in?"

There was that award-winning smile again as he stood and strode naked to the kitchen. My assurance faltered. He was *on* again—that shift between the mask and the man beneath. I tried to push down the lingering doubt that I was the only one who wanted this to be something more than physical, but his ability to maintain complete control the second the moment was over was unnerving.

CHAPTER 14

Frank

She was good.

I mean, she was *amazing.*

She felt incredible. Her body, her skin, everything about her made me want to get drunk on her. She was everything I dreamed she'd be and more.

And I wanted more.

I had stood behind her, wearing only my boxers when she answered the door to collect the takeout, making the delivery guy highly uncomfortable as I stared him down. My arms were crossed, muscles flexing with irritation, and my lip turned up into a snarl, exposing my slightly sharp teeth as Charlotte beamed at the delivery man while she collected the food and paid him his tip.

I got a tip for you, *fuck off.*

As though he had heard my thoughts, the delivery man shot me a terrified look before shuffling down the hallway.

Kind of glad I didn't say it out loud, though. I have a feeling it sounded cooler in my head than it actually was.

As she turned, she smiled at me. "You're acting a bit jealous there, Mr. Blackman."

My irritation melted away, partially due to her, because just looking at her could do that to me, but also because I could hear the delivery guy down the hall stepping into the elevator. The further Charlotte was from other men, the better I felt.

Something had flicked on inside me. Fuck, I thought I was possessive *before*, now I was straight up territorial over Charlotte. Our physical connection had me like a raging bull, ready to charge at anyone who came near her. I wanted her to myself, chained to the bed, wanting me and me alone.

This feeling was new to me, and I wasn't sure if I liked it.

Uncrossing my arms, I took the takeout bag from her. The plastic handles were thin from the strain of the containers weighing it down. Following her toward the kitchen as she took out plates and cutlery, I watched her, noticing there were only a few of each on the otherwise stark shelves.

Charlotte cast me a glance as I took the

containers out of the bag. Our inability to settle on something we wanted had resulted in us ordering four different choices from the same restaurant—two types of pasta, a salad, and risotto. Charlotte joked about having leftovers for tomorrow night and two nights after that.

Obviously, she hadn't seen me eat.

I hadn't spoken much since we left the bedroom, apart from deciding on dinner, and she watched me, no doubt wanting to know what thoughts were running through my mind.

I'll tell you right now, whatever she thought I was thinking was probably much more complicated than what I was actually thinking.

Food.

Sex.

Yum.

We sat on the couch since she didn't have a dining room table yet. Charlotte folded her legs underneath her, leaning against the arm and watching me while I put my feet up on the cardboard box that was currently acting as her coffee table, and from the sound of it, clothes were still in it. If she were searching me for any judgment for the state of her apartment, she wouldn't find any.

Sure, I surrounded myself with expensive things. But why not? I earned them.

I also had a reputation to keep.

"In five years, I'd like to be an architect," she said.

"Sorry?" I looked up from my food. She giggled, commenting that I ate like a teenage boy, shoveling it into my mouth as if it was my last meal. I still had a fork full of pasta, halfway between the plate and my mouth when she had turned to me.

"You asked me where I saw myself in five years. That's what I want to do."

I finished my mouthful, nodding. "Ah, and that's why you wanted to work for me because of the track history of my previous employees."

There was a history of those who had worked for me going on to do great things. Previous employees of mine had started three other architectural businesses, and while none of them were the conglomerate that Blackman, Conner, & Associates was, they were doing quite well for themselves. She nodded, and I smiled with the corner of my mouth—I had suspected as much.

"I think I need to start taking down my competition. People will think I'm soft if I keep launching other people's careers."

She laughed. "You're not soft."

"You would know."

My expression darkened as I looked at her, and she flushed under my gaze. She didn't look away, and I think she was trying to regain some of the dominance she had lost in the bedroom.

Maybe she was just daring me to take her again.

"So, you're sleeping your way to the top," I said, going back to my food.

"Don't joke about that. You know I'm concerned about having crossed that line."

I shrugged. "Your secret is safe with me."

As we finished eating, I asked about her ideas. She told me her visions for office buildings and homes, and interior design, and I was actually impressed. I joked about not wanting to lose my assistant, and she responded only with a skeptical look.

Like she was still trying to figure me out.

Honestly, it wasn't that hard. Apart from the obvious big secret, I was fairly open and honest. She kept looking at me like I was having these in-depth thoughts about whatever she was thinking.

All I was thinking of was her.

Sounds sweet, right?

No, that's complication.

Because there was a bond that had been cemented the moment I had penetrated her. Because whatever it was about her that brought out this side of me, I still hadn't unlocked it.

Charlotte

After loading the dishwasher, I sat back down, pulling Frank's shirt around my otherwise naked body. He had insisted I wear it, and his eyes had raked up and down my body, flashing with a possessiveness that from Joshua would've made me ill, but from him made my legs weak.

"Can I get you another drink?" Frank asked. When I nodded, he made his way into the kitchen, opening and closing cupboards at random until he found the glasses before returning to the couch with a bottle of wine. While I sat on the couch surrounded by the thoughts of the web I had managed to tangle myself in, I wondered how on earth I was going to get control of this situation.

Especially when I was so out of control with him.

"Were you saving this for any special occasion?" he asked, his hands poised to open the bottle. When I shook my head, he unscrewed the top and poured us both generous portions, sitting down next to me and handing me a glass.

I studied him. There were so many things I wanted to say, and yet I didn't say anything at all. I could feel the nervous energy building in my stomach. There was no going back now. It wasn't so much regret, it was more confusion as to where do we go from here? Did we continue working together as though nothing had happened? I didn't fancy being a secret mistress, but the exposure of any kind of our relationship—if that's what this was—would ruin our professional images. Although, I felt I'd suffer more from the equation.

I'd be cast as just another woman who couldn't resist Frank Blackman, while his career would continue without scathe.

I looked up from my wine to find him staring at me.

"What are you thinking?" I asked.

"I'm thinking about kissing you."

I let him take the practically untouched wine from my hand, and he placed both glasses on the floor by the side of the couch. Reaching forward, he pulled me onto his lap, hooked my panties in his thumb, and pulled them off as I straddled him. While he had put his boxers on before our dinner was delivered, he hadn't bothered with any other clothes, and his skin was warm where it touched my thighs, making me tingle against his skin.

I couldn't help it.

I'm in so much trouble.

Frank

Generally, women were easy to read.

I could always tell when they wanted me and what they wanted me to do. I could make them purr and squirm under my touch, and I certainly didn't need to keep asking them if they were enjoying it or if I were doing it right.

So, how to explain my constant need to hear her

say it?

Placing a hand on the back of her neck, I guided her lips toward mine and stopped before kissing her, gripping her neck when she tried to close the gap between us.

"Tell me you want me," I said.

"I want you, Frank."

Only then did I kiss her, my tongue sliding into her mouth as I tasted the wine on her. I decided red wine and Charlotte's lips were a good pairing. She was intoxicating in the best of ways, and she melted into my touch as I guided her head with my hand.

This constant desire to have her reaffirm her want for me was something new, and I wasn't sure how I felt about it. With her, I wanted to hear it. I wanted her to say my name and tell me over and over again how much she wanted me.

Confidence wasn't the issue, but something between us had me asking and had a spark igniting in my chest every time she confessed how much she wanted me.

"Where do you want me?" I asked against her lips.

She shifted on my lap, practically grinding against me like a horny teenager. "I want you inside of me."

I grinned, a smile that promised danger because she was in trouble now. I ran my hands down from her shoulders and pulled the shirt off as my fingers worked their way down her back. She moved her arms and allowed me to expose her until she was naked on my lap.

As my hands trailed down over her, I smirked. "You need to be more specific. You want me inside of you, and you have more than one entrance."

Charlotte gasped as my forefinger found her rear entrance, rubbing in small circles around the sensitive skin. She tensed. "Frank, please, I've never..." She added hastily, "I want you to fuck my pussy."

I continued to rub in small circles, her words had me biting my bottom lip. "Never?"

She shook her head, her brows knotted together as I pushed my finger inside, just a little bit, to the first joint. She could take it. My cock twitched when I felt her clench around my finger, her eyes closed with that gorgeous frown on her face while she got used to the intrusion.

"I want to take you... everywhere..."

"Please..." she whispered.

Was she asking me to stop or begging for more? The smile never left my face, that satisfaction at having her completely at my mercy. I lifted her off my lap slightly, bringing her to her knees, using my hand on her ass and my finger inside her to guide her movement. With my free hand, I tugged down my boxers, my eyes never leaving her face. I didn't want to miss a moment of the delectable torture her slight frown alluded to. Taking my time again and reaching between her legs, I traced lines of anticipation around her thighs until I heard those mewing sounds from her lips.

She was gyrating her hips again, perhaps subconsciously, so desperate for my touch that she was relaxing against the intrusion of my finger. I sunk a finger into her waiting warmth, rubbing her clit with my thumb before adding a second finger into her pussy, letting her ride my palm.

"Frank..." She squirmed under my touch, unable to get completely lost in the pleasure I was bringing her because of the intrusion in her ass.

But I kept my hand curved around her cheek and my finger just inside her entrance while I ignored her body's attempts to push me out as she clamped and twitched. I groaned with each spasm of her muscles, unable to control myself from sinking my finger into the second joint. She cried out, and I moaned openly.

God help me, she was so fucking tight. I could feel my control slipping.

I could imagine that tightness around my cock, squeezing the cum from me as I bent her over the couch or the mahogany desk in my office.

Removing my fingers from her pussy, I gripped her hip, lowering her onto me, poising my cock at her entrance. She was dripping with arousal, begging for me with the responses from her body.

"I think you like it," I muttered, holding her thigh and gripping to stop her from moving too fast. Her face scrunched again as I penetrated her, that delicious stretch consuming her.

I lowered her onto me, slowly and deliberately, until with her straddling me, I was fully sheathed inside her. Groaning as I bottomed out, her muscles clenched around my cock. Watching her face was ecstasy in itself—it was hard not to be smug about her expression as I stretched her. I knew I had a stupid grin plastered on my face as I took in the frown on hers. The way her lips stayed perpetually parted, those sounds I loved so much tumbling from her. Moving her up and down on me, I used my finger inside her and hand on her cheek to guide her movements.

"It's too tight," she whispered.

"Too tight for my finger? Imagine my cock in that ass," I whispered.

She whimpered.

Fuck.

"It won't fit…"

My voice went dark. "It'll fit."

My finger moved in further until I was buried up to my knuckle, making her cry out again.

She rested her forehead against mine as I started thrusting up into her, unable to control myself with the steady pace any longer. I wanted to hear her scream, to cry out my name.

As she leaned forward, her necklace dangled between us. I watched the cross sway above her breasts and growled, moving forward to take her nipple in my mouth. Something about what the cross represented angered me. She felt she was protected by it, but the only protection she needed, she could get from me.

Because she was mine now, and no one else could touch her.

I wondered who would protect her from *me*.

Charlotte began riding me, bracing her hands on the back of the couch and bouncing her hips so she was meeting my thrusts. I worked my tongue and teeth with controlled, gentle strokes and nips around her nipple, dragging little squeals of pleasure from her lips. I wanted to take her in every way, to watch my cock sink in between those lips after she begged, then bend her over and fuck her pussy over and over again until she could think of nothing but me. Maybe I'd try to slide my cock into that virgin ass of hers and take everything from her.

Because she belonged to me now.

I groaned at the thought, tilting my head back against the couch and pounding into her. "Fuck, you feel so good."

Opening my eyes, I watched her move above me.

Then I felt it.

This was more than just sex.

I knew.

I'm in trouble.

Something was changing within her. She was coming undone, more than the first time we'd fucked. It was like she was on the verge of breaking free of whatever was inside her that was holding her back, but she couldn't quite do it.

I wrapped an arm around her waist, pulling her against me so the friction stimulated her clit with every thrust. She started crying out—*loud*—the sort of volume I knew she'd never consciously reach. She'd be too concerned with how it appeared to her neighbors. I grinned against her breast. I *wanted* her to lose control with me the way I did with her.

Yes, let the world know who owns you.

When I started moving my finger in tandem with my thrusts, she screamed as she was pushed over the edge, and I felt her pulsate around my cock as she came. I could no longer hold back and sunk in deeper as I came with her.

CHAPTER
15

Charlotte

After our romp on the couch, we had made our way back into the bedroom, where Frank had taken me once more before we slept. I was just as eager as he to go again and crawled onto the bed, bending over in front of him. He had growled as he penetrated my pussy from behind, pushing a hand between my shoulder blades and forcing my face into the pillows as he took me.

I could make him lose control, and I liked having that power.

As the sunlight peeked around the heavy curtains, the bed protested as Frank dropped his weight onto the edge of the mattress, shaking me awake and handing me a coffee. I sat up, and he smirked as I stretched. Pulling my elbows toward each other behind my back, the move pushed my breasts out. I watched as his face darkened and only just managed to contain my smile. Sipping the coffee, I was pleasantly surprised at the smooth taste and wondered how he conjured it up using what he found in the pantry. It tasted like it had a sweet spice added to it. I hummed my approval as I settled against the pillows and took another sip.

Not a bad way to start a morning.

Lifting his legs onto the bed and lying next to me, he folded one arm behind his head.

"Guess I'm going to need to look for another assistant," he said.

I sat bolt upright, saving myself at the last moment before spilling my coffee over my new bedsheets. "What? Why?" I spluttered.

Surely, I misheard.

Frank looked at me, his brow furrowed at my reaction. "Because if we're going to be together, you won't need to work."

"I'm sorry. *What?*" Frank gave me a look that suggested I was overreacting, and when he opened his mouth to reply, I cut him off. "You're serious, aren't you? Even after I told you last night what I wanted to do with my career?"

"Well, yes." He stared at me, one eyebrow cocked, his expression otherwise blank. "What did you think was going to happen? That we'd go back to working together?"

His eyes flashed as my jaw dropped, almost like

he was daring me to contradict him. I knew last night when I asked him for us to keep it professional, it wasn't entirely realistic. I'm not an idiot. I knew it was just a thread I was clinging to, to justify fulfilling these desires I had kept banked up for so long.

But I hadn't expected him to do this.

"First of all," I carefully put the coffee on the bedside table, trying to maintain my composure, telling myself we could talk this through like adults. "I didn't assume that just because we had sex, we'd be in a relationship. Don't get me wrong, I like you, and I'd love to try making *us* a thing, but you don't *own me*. I came here to build myself a career, and I'm not going to give that all up because you earn more than me."

"I could buy and sell you."

Honestly, it felt as though he had slapped me.

He retreated, seeing the change in my face. "I didn't mean it that way."

I'd never seen him backtrack on anything he had said before, but the significance of this was lost in that moment. Through gritted teeth, I replied, "I think you said *exactly* what you meant."

"Charlotte—"

"I think you should leave." I stood and grabbed my dress from the night before, desperate not to be naked but not wanting to rifle through boxes of yet unpacked clothes. "Please leave."

"Stop!"

His shout startled me, and I glared at him. "I don't need your permission to get dressed."

He stood angrily, making his way around the bed as I stayed frozen on the spot. His body language screamed danger as he stopped in front of me, close enough I could feel the brush of his heated breath against my hair. The contrast between our body language now and our body language last night was not lost on either of us, I suspect. "Yes. You do need my permission," he growled, grabbing my dress and wrestling it from my grip as easily as if I were a child.

The show of strength should've frightened me, but instead, it just increased my anger, and as much as I hated to admit, it turned me on.

"Don't go treating me like you own me. If you want to be with me, we can give it a go, but you are *not* the boss of my entire life, and I'll not be some kept mistress. You can either accept that or you can leave." I was getting worked up. I could feel it, but I couldn't help it. Everything I worked for was unraveling in front of my eyes. This is *exactly* what I didn't want to happen. "I don't want to be forced out of my job. I enjoy it, and I can't afford this apartment without it."

"I'll buy it for you."

"I don't want you to do that. Why don't you understand?"

He was standing so close to me, breathing heavily, I could feel the heat from his body and ignored my internal urge to touch him, to comfort him, like he was the one needing comforting right now.

"I misread you." He threw my dress to the side, and for a moment, I thought he was going to touch me again. The way his eyes flickered between mine and a twitch of the hand, I braced myself as though he was going to toss me on the bed the way he had last night. Maybe then he'd apologize and make everything right.

His hands hovered near my body.

But he didn't touch me.

When he instead snatched his clothes from the floor, I felt the rejection flood over me like a wave that crashed over my body and broke my heart on the way down.

He growled. "All I wanted was to look after you, and you can't even accept that." As he stalked toward the door, he turned. "I'll see you Monday." Slamming the door behind him, he left me feeling completely exposed, having nothing to do with my nudity.

CHAPTER 16

Charlotte

To say the atmosphere in the office on Monday was cold would be an understatement.

But I learned something valuable about my co-workers—either they were incredibly unobservant, or they genuinely didn't care about my change in attitude. I thought the switch between Frank and me before and after the conference was noticeable, but maybe small enough to be too subtle for those not in the inner circle not to see.

But this? This was night and day, light and dark.

Everything about our body language had changed, including the stiff tones we now used to acknowledge each other.

Everything had changed.

This realization shifted something in me, and now it was all about business. I usually tried to be friendly with co-workers. We didn't have to go out together and catch up after work, but you could still be friends with those you worked with.

But there was nothing now, no motivation to treat these people with any warmth.

They treated me exactly the same as when I started, which told me they were co-workers only and would never be anything more. I had no desire to interact with anyone beyond the strictly professional, and I spoke to Frank in clipped tones, ending every sentence in a drawl bordering on sarcasm with *sir* or *Mr. Blackman.*

I took a certain level of pride in how much this seemed to piss him off.

This controlling relationship shit, this is what I came here to get away from. I was not going to step out of one relationship with a man who wanted me to be a housewife and run straight into the arms of another.

I had told Frank all of this, and the fact that he still didn't get it spoke worlds to me.

Only I figured it out too late.

One year in this job, maybe two, and I could move on to bigger and better things and forget this place and everyone in it.

I could do that, no problem.

It was a lie, but I wouldn't admit that to myself.

Frank

She was going about her day, and I watched her move around the office. I could barely concentrate, my every sense extra receptive to her. I could smell her skin beyond her perfume and feel my fingers in her hair whenever I watched her brush it behind her ears, and could almost feel the smear of her lipstick against my abdomen. By even alluding to a relationship with Charlotte and telling her I wanted to look after her, I had stepped way beyond my comfort zone. In my own way, it had been a big step.

I thought maybe she'd have realized that. Guess I thought wrong.

I had offered her the world—my world—and she had thrown it back in my face.

Demons had two emotions—fuck or fight.

If she didn't want to fuck me, then a fight it was.

It seemed in one way or another, I was drawn to her. Whether through anger or lust, the feelings were just as strong and gripped at my organs, twisting them whenever she spoke to me in that flat monotone before walking away. I was *sure* she was wiggling her hips more than necessary, like waving a red flag at a raging bull.

What would she do if I charged at her, taking her right on the office floor and proving to her that I *was* her boss here and everywhere?

Staying steadfast in my conviction that I had

done nothing wrong, I had tried to see it from her point of view, but I kept coming back to the same conclusion.

She was overreacting.

Hell, the fact I was *trying* to see it from her point of view was more than I'd normally bother with.

What had she done to me?

I hadn't done anything wrong by being with her, for clearly, she wanted me as much as I did her, and I certainly hadn't done anything wrong in wanting to look after her. Why should she have to work when I made enough to keep us both comfortable? She could stay at home, going out and doing as she pleases, as long as she was there in the evenings to greet me at the door, naked and ready for me to unleash.

Drumming my fingers against my desk, my impatience was displayed openly, and *fuck*, if she wanted to *talk* about her day and hear about mine, then I could offer that too. I was acutely aware that, even to myself, this confession made me question how much of my demon was still in control.

Look at what she had done to me—weakened me with these *feelings* and then rejected me.

I hadn't felt intense satisfaction with any human woman before as I had with her, and demon women, well they were great, but they could get violent, and fighting for every fuck got tiresome after a while.

But if Charlotte wanted to play games, well, I could play hard.

Calling Charlotte into my office later that week, I tilted back in my chair. Irritation radiated from me while she took her time finishing whatever-the-fuck task she was working on and striding into my office in her own time. She came and stood to my left as she always did, expecting to be handed some paperwork or files. So, when I stood, she startled, finding that with only the slightest step forward, I'd be pressed against her.

I towered over her, and my dark eyes dared her to move.

Run so that I can chase you.

But she didn't move, staying steadfast and staring up at me. I sneered.

A challenge.

Reaching down, I pulled two neckties from my desk drawer. "Which one for the client dinner tonight?" I asked, holding them under my chin in the small space between us.

Charlotte studied the ties without looking at my face, her expression feigning a disinterest that didn't convince me. I could feel the heat coming from her skin and heard how her heart rate increased when I stood. She wasn't fooling me.

"The charcoal one," she said, pointing the one on the left with a subtle paisley pattern embroidered into it.

I nodded. "You can help me tie it, please. I hurt my hand the other day."

She frowned at me, and I waved my hand around limply. She knew exactly what I was doing. She hadn't been close enough to touch me since I was in her home.

She also knew I was a fast healer.

And a liar when I wanted to be.

She scoffed and snatched the tie from my hand, ignoring my victory grin as she worked to remove the tie I was wearing. Once removed, she didn't put it in my open palm, instead dropping it resolutely on the desk behind me, and all without giving me the eye contact I silently demanded of her. I stood waiting, baiting her to move as she poised her hands near my chest, her flicker of hesitation all too clear.

Wrapping the silky fabric around my neck, Charlotte positioned the tie to knot it. I grunted when she tugged forward on both sides, under the ruse of straightening it but intending to do exactly as she did—yank hard against the back of my neck. I didn't budge and said nothing, but my eyes flashed with anger. I'll be honest, I felt a hint of pride at her silent rebellion.

Expertly, she finished the knot and tightened it around my neck. She glared at me as she tightened it further, but I didn't say anything. She kept going until the knot was pushing against my Adam's apple, and even though I had to adjust my breathing, I didn't flinch.

But I did lose control for a second, and something that was almost a quiet groan built in my throat.

Her eyes widened, and I knew she had realized her mistake too late.

I liked it.

Harder.

She made a sound that could've been a moan, but then she cleared her throat as she readjusted the knot again, loosening it appropriately and patting it with her fingers before taking a step back to admire her handiwork. Her eyes raked over the rest of my body, and I smirked.

"Is that all… *sir*?"

I took a step closer to her, closing the gap she had just made between us. "Didn't I ask you to call me Frank?"

"I guess you did."

"So, you're disobeying me?"

Charlotte's jaw dropped before she corrected herself, and I grinned.

I bent slightly until my lips were at her ear. "And

what if I told you I like it when you call me *sir?*"

She gasped, then glared at me, stalking out of the office while I chuckled. I could read her every movement, almost her every thought. Whatever the inexplicable connection we had, which we had cemented the other night, she still felt it too, and she hated when I got the upper hand on her.

She may have been stubborn, but she had no idea who she was dealing with.

CHAPTER
17

Charlotte

Showing Andy around the business, I tried to ignore Frank's stares as we passed by his office.

"He's a bit intense, isn't he?" Andy asked, twisting his hands together.

I laughed. "Mr. Blackman? He's fine. You don't need to be afraid of him."

"I'm not afraid." But the look he threw over his shoulder as if he was expecting to find Frank hiding in the shadows told another story.

When I finished the office tour, I showed Andy to his cubicle and desk. He was one of the new team hired to help with the skyline project that would really put Blackman, Conner & Associates on the map. Andy smiled as I confirmed that he knew where everything was.

"Thank you, Charlotte, you've been very helpful."

"Any time, and if you need anything, my speed dial is on your phone."

Shaking his hand, the corner of my lip twitched as his touch lingered. I was almost certain he was flirting with me, whether because of the air of sex that seemed to follow around me since my night with Frank or because I had taken to wearing dresses specifically to bother my *boss*, I wasn't sure.

I also didn't care.

I had no interest in going there with a co-worker again and shouldn't have in the first place. If my experience with Frank had taught me anything, it had only cemented what a bad idea it was.

But a harmless flirt never hurt anyone, and Andy seemed like a genuinely nice guy. Almost too nice to be working in a place where professionalism trumps all else, including noticing if your co-workers are dealing with some personal shit. From our brief chat, I knew that Andy loved music, played guitar, and I got the impression that the Andy in the office would be a different person from the Andy at the bar.

Not that I ever planned on finding out.

But it was fun to let Frank think I would.

Frank watched me again as I sat down. I noticed him stand from the corner of my eye, and I deliberately turned away from him to do some filing, so he had to walk around my desk.

"New team settling in okay?" he asked.

Looking up at him, I beamed brightly. "Yes, *sir*."

A nerve twitched in Frank's brow, looking like he had a hundred retorts he was biting back. As he went back to his desk, I released a slow breath.

Pretending you were in control was exhausting.

Andy was in the kitchenette, stirring a coffee when I came in to fill my water bottle.

"Nice day, huh?"

I smiled without turning around, waiting for the bottle to be full before I straightened and leaned my hip against the counter.

"Seriously? We're going to talk about the weather?" I asked, smirking.

"It started a conversation, didn't it?"

I returned his grin. "I guess I can't argue with that. How are you settling in?"

"Good, good, really good."

"Good." I chuckled, "Good, *good*."

He laughed again, a gentle, easy sound. He wasn't embarrassed. Apparently, he was more confident within himself than I had given him credit for. "It's a challenging role. I needed that in my life."

"A challenge?"

"I never turn away from a challenge." He winked.

I raised an eyebrow at him, definitely confident.

"Some challenges are worth the effort."

While he was still leering at me, his eyes never left my face. He didn't rake his gaze up and down my body the way Frank did, but he also didn't bring out that longing to be touched the way Frank did either.

Why was I comparing him to Frank?

I didn't need to ask myself because I knew. Frank had become the pillar of perfection in my mind, and the man who had ruined me for all other men. I'd be forever asking myself if the next man could stretch me like Frank did, push me to my limits, and bring me to a screaming orgasm.

Or make me feel so safe, so protected and understood.

Dammit.

A night out—that's what I needed.

At least, that is what Meredith had decided for me, partially to distract me from *The Frank Debacle,* as she called it. Apparently, I needed to *get Frank out of my system,* Meredith had announced using finger quotations.

She wasn't wrong.

Meredith had also been quick to point out that I still didn't have many friends in the city beyond herself. I knew Meredith's friends but not well enough to consider them my own and not enough to call on them if I needed a chat. This is something Meredith was determined to fix, and I had to admit, I did appreciate it. I missed having a group of girlfriends I could go to. I had lost all of that, not when I moved, but before that, because of Joshua.

Joshua—who was now just an insignificant speck in my mind compared to the cavern that Frank occupied there.

That left me squeezed into the back of the cab with Meredith and Erica.

"All I'm saying..." Meredith continued with a wink, "... is don't rule it out."

Erica laughed, a dark laugh to match her hair and eyes. She had a voice that would do her well if she were to get involved in an erotic phone chat job, but I said nothing about it, sure she'd heard it all before.

I smiled. "I'm not having a one-night stand tonight."

"It might do you good," Erica added. There was no condescension in her tone, only a hint of humor. She had heard the short version of my *situation* with Frank, tutting while a smirk adorned her face when she found out he was my boss.

We tumbled out of the cab when the driver pulled up in front of the club. I was ready to head to the back of the short line when Erica cupped her hand around the bouncer's cheek and whispered something in his ear. His face remained stoic, mostly, until a hint of a break in his demeanor presented before he laughed and waved us in. I wanted to ask what she had said to him, but my eardrums were assaulted by the music the moment we opened the door and crossed the threshold.

The bass pounded against the inside of the club, threatening to tear it apart, as a mass of sweaty, gyrating bodies covered the generous dance floor. This was not the sort of place you came to talk, to sit and have a quiet conversation about your feelings. This was where you came to have a drink—or two or more—and allow the music to force every thought from your mind except the present moment.

Two rounds of shots later, and we were on the dance floor with Phoebe and Daniella, keeping our circle enclosed and focusing on each other. Initially, I hadn't understood how Meredith expected me to get to know the other girls when we could barely hear each other talk. It had been so long since I'd had anything that resembled a girls' night, apparently, I had almost forgotten how to do it.

Almost.

But there was something about this sort of club,

something about moving close, laughing at each other's silly dance moves, swapping compliments, and building each other up that was bonding.

When a group of men made their way across the dance floor, only one of the three at least attempting to dance his way toward us rather than straight-up striding, Meredith grinned at me. The men introduced themselves, their names immediately lost in the music, and no one caring enough to repeat them before joining our circle.

He was tall but not as tall as Frank. His body was leaner, as though he chose cardio over weights. I smirked when I noticed he was checking me out as much as I was him. It was hard not to with him so close, the intoxication from the bass and the vodka swirling in my system. He had gray eyes, and I couldn't tear mine away. So when he moved closer and placed his hands on my waist, his legs intertwining with mine, and we started moving together, I didn't protest.

I kept watching his eyes, and he didn't break the eye contact, even beyond the point I thought it was considered impolite to stare. I wanted to know his name.

Or maybe I didn't.

Maybe all I needed was this moment—a reminder that Frank wasn't the only man out there. Although, I was waiting for the chills up my spine at this man's touch.

They didn't come.

The way his thumb caressed just under my ribs as he kept his hands on my waist, not trying to cop a cheap feel but coupled with the leer on his face, told me all I needed to know about his intentions.

I just wanted to dance and get lost in this moment.

That's all.

For tonight, that was enough.

CHAPTER
18

Charlotte

When I stepped around the corner to my office to check my phone, I let the fake smile drop from my face I'd had plastered on all night. The sounds from the client party in the boardroom muted slightly as I rounded the second corner and leaned against the wall. I was tiring of this game with Frank, and from the way he looked at me, watching me from the corner of his eye as he listened to the latest stories of success from his employees and the client's satisfaction with their work, I could tell he was tiring of it too.

The question was, who would break first?

Sighing, I placed my phone on my desk and prepared to return to the party. Initially thrown to celebrate a successful quarter—as Frank and Mike believed that rewards and happiness made for better workers—but a few key clients were invited. Perhaps to show off the work environment as much as keep them happy. Either way, there was an image to be kept up. Straightening my clothes and putting on my best *everything-is-okay* simper, I turned.

And walked straight into Frank's chest.

"You've been ignoring me," he said through gritted teeth as I straightened.

"I haven't been ignoring you, I've been treating you as my boss." I met his eyes, regretting the moment I did, as once again, his eyes flared with that possessive nature. "I have a job to do."

It had been another long week of keeping up appearances, of pretending that he wasn't getting to me as much as I could tell I was getting to him. On top of that, Andy had asked me out, and I'd had to turn him down. His reaction upset me more than my feelings because I had completely blocked myself off from any chance with him since he was a co-worker, but it still wasn't fun to reject him.

Frank moved forward until I was backed against the wall that separated my desk from the rest of the office floor. There was no door, just a corner L-shaped wall which anyone could walk around at any time. I whispered his name urgently, putting my hands on his chest.

Which was a mistake.

He looked down at me.

I wasn't pushing him away, just touching him.

"Have you slept with him?"

Anger flared in me again. "Who?"

"Andy." Frank's eyes flashed dangerously as he said the name.

"What? No! Of course not," I huffed out. "Not that it's any of your business who I sleep with." I rubbed my arms, looking to the side and trying to ignore how close he was to me. "Besides, if I wanted to, I would. He's nice to me."

"*I'm* nice to you," Frank snarled the words.

"You just try to control me," I snapped.

With a half-step forward, Frank pressed his body against mine, crushing me against the wall. I let out an involuntary moan, biting my bottom lip to stifle further sound as a dark sneer crossed Frank's face.

"You like it when I control you."

Gasping, I was prepared to be offended but unable to find it within myself to argue the truth with him. I didn't speak, hoping that my face didn't betray the growing wetness between my legs, aching for his fingers, his tongue, and his cock.

My breathing came in unsteady gasps as his body pressed against mine. His erection pressed against my stomach through his pants. Looking at the ceiling, I squeezed my eyes shut for a moment.

God help me, I wanted him.

Then he did something that completely floored me.

He *apologized.*

And it took me a second to clear my head.

It may have been a forced apology, but it was still an apology. He was *trying*. That, coupled with another confession about his thoughts about me, only made this harder to fight. There was something in him, something that crawled beneath his skin that made me feel as though I could take on the world. It was more than sex, it was power. It was a complete confidence in who I was and what I could achieve. Despite our *disagreement*, when we talked, he encouraged me to be the best I could be. He pushed me, both inside the office and out, and showed me just how incredible life could really be.

Frank

As I pressed against her, I could feel her stubbornness. I wanted her, and I always got what I wanted. My demon fumed as the rage built inside me. This close to her, I could smell another man on her. She didn't smell of sex, and it wasn't only Andy's scent, which means she had been out last weekend. Maybe she had a drink with a stranger, danced with him, maybe he kissed her. The thoughts drove me crazy with the need to reclaim her as my own.

I tried to think, huffing heavily to clear my

nostrils of other men's scents. Maybe this time it couldn't be entirely on my terms, and I needed to consider how she, *for fuck's sake, felt.*

Compromise was not something I was good at.

My teeth were still gritted as I spoke. "I'm sorry I tried to make you quit, but no one else has responded to me the way you did, and I can't stop thinking about it. I only wanted to do what was best for you."

She had her eyes closed, and they snapped open at my words. I could almost see her resolve melting behind her eyes. I moved closer, as close as I could possibly be while we were both clothed, and I wasn't penetrating her.

Yet.

"We shouldn't do this," she murmured.

I wasn't sure if she was telling herself or me.

"Maybe we shouldn't." My stare was hard as I leaned in further, dropping my voice. "Tell me you don't want me, tell me you don't feel it, and I'll walk away right now."

I meant it. It wouldn't be easy, but I meant it.

She looked into my dark eyes, her voice barely a whisper, although no one could hear us over the music anyway. "I can't tell you that because I want you."

I was on her.

My hands pulled at the top so neatly tucked into her skirt, my lips on hers, teeth on teeth as I hungrily took her mouth. When she put her hands on my chest again, I took both her wrists in my fist and held them above her head, pinning her against the wall. Using my free hand to cover her mouth, I kissed and nipped my way down her neck and over the exposed top of her breasts, nibbling at the lace on her bra.

"Right now," I grunted out. "I need you right now." Then my hands were yanking up her skirt and undoing my fly, freeing myself from the confines of my clothes. Charlotte cast a look toward the wall, one foot of stone the only barrier between the rest of the staff and us.

"We can't."

"I can do whatever the fuck I want."

"Frank—"

"*Now.*"

Hoisting her up onto my hips, I hooked my arms under her legs until she was opened to me, and guided my cock inside her waiting wetness, forcing the thin fabric of her panties to the side. I could smell other men on her, just from her being near them at the party, and it was driving me crazy. Unable to control myself long enough to allow her the luxury, I didn't give her time to adjust to my size. Not this time. I began rutting against her, long, deep, hard thrusts that kept her pinned between me and the wall as I barely kept control of my strength.

She's mine.

Resting my face in the crook of her neck and shoulder, I fucked her against the wall, thankful that the building was built well lest I fuck her through it. She was held up only by her legs and the power of my thrusts, my cock buried deep inside her. Charlotte bit down on her hand to stop herself from screaming out as I grunted, pushing myself into her and forcing her body to open up to me again and again. Her legs twitched—maybe she was getting sore. But the ache must have been sweet as she moaned into her hand, gripping onto the collar of my shirt, and pulling me to her.

"Touch yourself," I mumbled. When she only moaned in response, I pushed in deeper, burying my cock until my hips met her thighs. I repeated the command and moaned against her when she moved her hand between her legs and started rubbing her clit.

Burying my face in her cleavage, I licked and kissed and nipped at her. With a particularly deep thrust, my teeth sunk into her flesh, making her eyes widen and causing Charlotte to bite her lip to stop herself from crying out. My sharp teeth had broken her skin, and I mumbled an apology against her as I kept my face buried between her breasts, not breaking momentum as I thrust into her.

I could smell the blood, *her blood*, tiny droplets forming around my teeth marks on her skin. I wanted to taste her, to swallow her blood and let it infect my system.

I shouldn't, though. It had been so long.

A long time ago, I had taken more than my share and almost took the life of the host as a result.

But one taste of her, just one little bit, surely wouldn't send me back down that path. I was older now, more controlled, and I wouldn't hurt her. As my tongue found the droplets of blood on her breast, my pupils dilated, and I spasmed inside her.

"How do you feel now?"

I looked down, watching my fingers turn the silver cross over, studying the details of it.

"Better," I replied, breathing out heavily. I looked up at the priest, his eyes a clear blue, full of calming and truth. I liked this priest. I didn't like the other one, he was older and harsher. But this one, with his younger face, round but handsome, and sandy blond hair that fell in front of his eyes, he spoke to me as though I were an adult and not a child.

"The pain you've been experiencing, the cross will help you, along with faith in God."

"What's wrong with me?" I asked, hating the way my voice sounded as though it verged on tears. I wouldn't cry again. I'd spent so long crying already. Crying when no one believed me about the attack, then crying when the cramps took over my stomach and legs. Crying when they finally did

believe me when the doctor saw the bite marks on my underdeveloped breasts and thighs, then crying when they dragged me into the church. Those cries turned into screams when the word exorcism *had been thrown around, only this young priest in front of me now to thank for that path not being followed.*

"You've been touched by the hand of the devil, but we will help you. That necklace has been blessed and will keep the devil out of your body. You must never take it off."

"My parents said they were going to send me away."

The priest nodded, his kind eyes understanding of my pain. "There is a school where they'll be able to make sure you stay safe."

My tears were real now, coming down my cheeks in steady streams. "I don't want to go away."

"It's what's best."

The priest's face faded behind my expanded pupils, and I was back in the office, my face buried between Charlotte's perfect breasts as she bounced on my cock.

"Frank," she whispered, "I'm so close."

My body responded to her words, and as she clamped around me, I came with her. My knees almost buckled as my body worked without my mind, seeking the pleasure that was nestled between her heavenly legs and pumping into her.

After a short while, she patted my back, and I lowered her to the floor. I watched blankly as she straightened her skirt and tucked her shirt back in. She beamed at me, her cheeks flushed and her hair messy, a sight that would usually mesmerize me. She was talking to me, but I couldn't focus on what she was saying. I stared straight through her, licking the remnants of her blood from my teeth. She saw the small break of the skin on her breast and brushed away the remaining droplets of blood, buttoning her shirt over the accidental wound brought on by a moment of passion.

I stared.

The metallic taste of her was still heavy in my mouth.

It all made sense now.

The unspoken connection between us that brought us together, the way we reacted to each other during sex, and the way that no matter how hard we tried, we were drawn together like magnets.

I had felt it, tasted it.

The memory wasn't mine, but through her life's blood, I had seen it as though it were.

"We need to talk, Charlotte," I said.

Charlotte smiled at me as she was combing her fingers through her hair. "Okay, but we need to get back to the party, people are going to get suspicious."

"Charlotte—"

"Follow me out in a couple of minutes."

Before I could answer, she had disappeared around the corner, returning to play her role in the party. My shoulders sunk. I didn't go back to the crowd but stalked into my office and sat at my desk with only the city lights to illuminate my troubled face.

I had tasted it in her blood.

Demon blood.

CHAPTER
19

Charlotte

Although Andy offered, Frank insisted on driving me home that night, but I was quite happy to take a cab. However, Frank had grabbed my arm as we walked out of the office. I was sure his grip was tighter than he intended, but he ignored my questioning look as he led me to his car, throwing Andy a scathing glare that left him shrinking against the wall as we entered the elevator.

I felt kind of bad for the guy.

It also excited me—*that power.*

But my enthusiasm evaporated when I looked at Frank, watching him drive. The muscles in his jaw were taut as he clenched his teeth. I slid down in my seat, not able to figure out what I had done that had angered him so much. He had taken me in a fit of passion, and I had responded, but since then, he hadn't spoken a word to me. In fact, he had barely looked at me.

If anything, this was worse than the forced professionalism we had been acting out.

The moment we crossed the threshold to my apartment, he had me backed up against the closed door, reaching around me and locking it.

My skin tingled.

I purred at him, "Frank—"

"Tell me about the attack."

"What?"

I was snapped out of the mood in the worst possible way, being dragged down into the memories I had been trying to push back since they began surfacing when I moved to the city. Watching his eyes, his expression darkened as he looked at me, every muscle tense as I shifted my gaze to his arms, boxing me in.

He was controlled, sort of.

He wasn't angry—he was upset.

I think I'd have preferred him to be angry.

I could see it in the way he looked at me, as though I were a doll, broken and discarded. I wasn't afraid of him or his strength, but he was holding something back from me, something that was torturing him, and that scared me more than anything.

"Tell me about the attack," he whispered, his voice hoarse. "Please."

"Why?" My voice was small.

Frank swallowed and looked away from me. When he looked back, there was a sorrow in his eyes that made my heart ache. I watched a muscle in his neck twitch as he kept whatever he was thinking to himself.

He licked his lips, then hesitated several times. Whatever it was he was trying to say, it was hard and painful for him. That definitely made it worse. This man *cared* for me. So much, in fact, that the idea of upsetting me was throwing him off more than any other situation I'd seen him in.

What the hell was going on?

Frank visibly steeled himself before asking, "Did he..." he licked his lips again, forcing the words out, "... drink your blood?"

I felt the memory of Frank's tongue on my skin, tasting the blood on my breast as he fucked me against the wall. When he asked that question, the thoughts flared within my mind, melting together with those from so long ago. I had been re-building the memories together for weeks. I didn't want to, but it forced itself together in the back of my mind until it was fully formed.

I didn't want to remember. Every piece that fell into place just made me think *no, I don't want to remember!*

But I had to.

I met Frank's eyes. "No," I whispered. "He made me drink his."

As I sank to the floor, I was weighed down as it all came back, all the memories of the attack in stark clarity and the weeks and months following—all the gaps filling in. They came forth from the darkest recesses of my mind, where they had laid dormant except for the nights they crawled out to sink their teeth into my dreams, twisting them into nightmares.

Frank lifted me under my arms and moved me to my bedroom. Sitting me on the edge of the bed, he removed my shoes and stockings with slow, purposeful actions, his fingers dragging across my skin in gentle movements. I watched his hands as he worked, handling me as if I were made of porcelain, and his touching me could make me fall apart more than the memories already had. There was nothing sexual about his touch, and somehow that made it worse that he thought the situation so desperate he needed to care for me like a child.

If Frank was scared, then I was terrified.

I lay down on the bed as he guided me, lifting

pillows behind my head and shoulders and kicking off his shoes before he crawled over me. Momentarily I was distracted by his closeness, but he didn't touch me, only carefully lifted himself over me before lying next to me. Resting his head on his hand, he lay on his side and faced me, his eyes darting between mine before raking across my face.

Lazily, I rolled my head to the side, watching him watch me. His eyes didn't stray from mine.

I didn't like this. I wanted it back to how it was the last time we were in bed before the strains of reality outside this bedroom had brought us down, and my past had come back to haunt me in a living, waking nightmare.

"Tell me about the attack, Charlotte," he said.

"What happened to me?" I whispered. Every moment brought back stronger flashes of memories as I wove them together in my mind like a tapestry.

I don't want to remember.

"Do you believe in God?" Frank asked after a beat.

I was snapped from my thoughts and pondered the question. It wasn't an easy one to answer. I had been raised religious, and it had played an important part in my life from Sunday school through to youth groups, and almost all of my social experiences had been through the church. But that had changed as I got older, and for a long time, I accepted that this was just a part of growing older and growing apart from my parents, given their outdated attitudes about a woman's role in life.

Now that these memories were swirling around in my mind and coming to the forefront, I was forced to remember in vivid detail, whereas previously, they had lived in the back of my mind, harmonious with my existence in denial. Now I was faced with this, I wondered when I turned my back on the church. Did I blame them for the boarding school? Did I blame my parents? Or both?

Was God still a part of my life? I supposed He was. I still spoke to Him, and not just in moments of pain or uncertainty. I still found solace in His presence in my heart and life, but I'd not consider myself to be practicing religion.

So, there was only one answer I could give. "Yes." I wanted to elaborate but found myself drained of energy. "Why do you ask?"

"If you believe in God, then you must believe in the Devil."

This was not the direction I had expected the conversation to take. Although, in saying that, I wasn't sure where he was going when he asked me about God in the first place. I knew I could have absolute trust in him, trust that he'd care for me, just like I trusted that no matter how rough he got in the bedroom, he would never seek to harm me.

"Yes," I said. "You can't have one without the other."

Frank nodded. "You're right, acceptance of the existence of God goes hand in hand with acceptance of the existence of the Devil. Therefore, angels and demons would be there too."

A small frown presented itself between my brows, and he held my gaze.

Slowly, I suspected I might know where he was going with this line of questioning, but that was impossible and ridiculous. Surely, a grown man wouldn't believe in such things. Those things only existed in the movies.

"Frank—" I started.

"Charlotte..." he cut me off. "You were attacked by a demon."

I just stared at him. Slowly, a smile curled on the corner of my lips. "Frank," I said again. "You can't be serious."

"There's not much I can do to convince you."

"You seriously believe that? That it was a demon and not just some psycho who got his kicks from twisted acts?"

Frank simply looked at me, his expression hadn't changed. He wasn't angry, upset, or disappointed, he was simply having a conversation with me. This made the grin drop from my lips.

To him, this wasn't a joke.

He actually believed what he said.

So either he was crazy, or I was.

"Frank..." I said again, whispering his name as though I were about to comfort him and explain that monsters didn't really exist in the real world.

But they did, I should know that.

They existed in the form of people, bad people who did bad things.

"Tell me about the attack, Charlotte. Please."

He wouldn't let up, and he already knew more than anyone else. When I was younger, no one would listen, not until I got sick. Preparing to tell Frank wasn't easy, not because of who he was to me—a friend, a lover—but because putting it into words would solidify the attack and make it real in a way that I had denied for years.

Something occurred to me, and I had to ask, "How did you know about the blood?"

Frank continued to stare at me. "Tell me everything."

CHAPTER
20

Frank

I just listened.

"I still don't know how I got into those woods, but I do know I was out with friends. They encouraged me to sneak out of my house. I'd never done it before, but there was a party, and some cute boys from school were going to be there. I wanted to talk to them because we never moved in the same circles since I was too quiet. I was sure if I could just talk to them, maybe one of them would like me, and it would change my life at school. I could be popular, cool, and not merely the child of the too strict parents, the girl never allowed out on weekends, the only teenager without a social life.

"When we arrived at the party, there was a group of older boys. One was the brother of one of my schoolmates and some of his friends.

"It wasn't long before I felt uncomfortable, and I wanted to go home. The girls said I was bringing the party down and told me to just leave. It wasn't far. It was a small town, and I could walk. It was a walk I had done a hundred times before. I had no reason to be afraid. It didn't occur to me I might be in danger. I was more scared of one of the older boys, who had white-blond hair and these piercing blue eyes. But the way he looked at me... you hear people say they were looked at like a piece of meat, but this was exactly that. It was like I wasn't a girl, not even human, but like I was prey to be caught and devoured, and he stared at me the entire time, and I thought if I left, that would be the end of it."

I didn't want to interrupt but couldn't help myself. "What sort of party was it?"

Charlotte waved a dismissive hand. "I don't think the party itself is important."

Staying silent, I decided it was better not to tell her how important the party itself may have been. If the demon made her drink his blood, then he had planned it and had intended to find someone. The party sounded like many others, a deliberate gathering of girls at exactly the right age—early to mid-teens—vulnerable and easy to manipulate.

Beyond that, if the demon had finished what he had started, if she hadn't had been put under the protection of the church and the boarding school, she'd have been no better than a slave to him—a submissive, compliant young woman who would give her life to him and for him when he tired of her.

I watched her as she talked, picturing what she might have looked like at that age and could see why the demon would have singled her out. Blonde hair and pale skin, I imagined she looked the exact personification of innocence.

Demons were incredibly territorial, and my instinct to bed Charlotte the moment we met was no coincidence. It was my body responding to the beginning of a claim by another demon. My protectiveness over her had not been helped by the fact that I genuinely got along with her. We could just sit and talk, have an actual intelligent conversation. I laughed with her, honestly laughed. The fact that we fit perfectly together, and the sex was incredible was quite simply a bonus.

I'd never had to explain about demons to anyone. There was a tiny flicker of doubt as I lay there, but every time I locked eyes with Charlotte, I wanted to give her all the answers. It wouldn't be easy for her, but she wouldn't be able to move forward with her life until she faced what had happened.

There was no easy way to reveal to her what I was, and considering that her past was haunted by a demon, the idea that the truth about me could tear us apart wasn't a reality I was willing to face.

Not yet.

She continued...

"So anyway, I left the party, and somehow, got lost. Then the streetlights started going out, and darkness took over the area. I couldn't see anything. I tried to run, and ended up in the woods...

"He was there.

"I started crying, asking him to let me go home, but he'd just laugh. I remember he was on top of me. One moment he was standing by the trees, and the next he was just on me, and those eyes, those yellow eyes glowed unnaturally in the night...

"I thought he was going to rape me, I was so scared. I hadn't even kissed a boy before. I remember sobbing and begging and trying to push him off me because wherever he touched me, it was like ice, that cold, stinging touch that was painful after only a few moments of contact and left my skin feeling like it had been burned.

"His tongue was on my neck, and he was touching me through my clothes, licking and biting at me. When he undid my jeans, he held me down with a hand on my chest, I was struggling so hard. He touched me...

"He looked at me with those yellow eyes, delighted. 'You're a virgin.'

"I pleaded, 'Please, please don't hurt me.'

"He withdrew his hand from my pants and licked his fingers, humming with a grating sound, like metal on metal.

"Then he undid his shirt, and using a fingernail,

he sliced into his chest. I screamed as his blood ran from the wound. He grabbed the back of my head and forced me into a sitting position as he straddled me, pushing my head against his chest.

"Taste it," he told me.

"I resisted and struggled some more, although, by then, I should've realized he was too strong for me. Then he held that bloody fingernail to my neck and told me if I didn't taste his blood, he'd cut into my throat, and he'd drink my blood until I was just an empty shell.

"So, I drank his blood.

"I don't remember much after that. I was found the next day, clothes shredded from a long night of wandering through the woods and no shoes. My parents didn't believe me. I wasn't raped or beaten, and no one at the party remembered the blond-haired man. There was no evidence, no signs, and I could tell the local police wanted to help, but even their eyes were skeptical. I was lost, dehydrated, and scared, so they said I must have had a nightmare.

"But then the urges started.

"I almost attacked my mother, snarling and clawing at her like an animal. She said my eyes went yellow... funny how my father believed her and not me. Then there were the cramps, those excruciating stomach pains that had me buckled over, but the doctors couldn't find anything wrong.

"So, when they didn't know what else to do, my parents took me to church. The eldest priest wanted to do an exorcism. Thankfully, my parents refused after another priest told them not to proceed. They were old-fashioned but not from the dark ages. The younger priest blessed my necklace and told me it would keep me safe as long as I never took it off. For good measure, they sent me to boarding school to finish my school years.

"As soon as I was eighteen, I left and went to college and got out of my parents' house as fast as I could. I blamed them. I didn't remember the attack, I just remembered them sending me away and that the school was so harsh and cold. It was no place for a young, vulnerable teenager.

"As the years went on, the memories faded until it was nothing more than a bad dream, a nightmare that haunted me only when I slept until the nightmares stopped.

"But then I moved here, and they came back, stronger than ever."

CHAPTER
21

Charlotte

Staring at Frank, I silently pleaded with him. His expression hadn't changed, and his eyes flitted between my face and the necklace I wore. I touched my neck, tracing my fingers down to my chest, remembering the feel of my attacker doing the same.

His eyes, *those yellow eyes.*

I was starting to panic. Reliving the experience had my heart gripped in a vice. I could feel the panic working its way up my body and into my lungs. I couldn't breathe. I clutched at my necklace, letting the silver dig into the flesh of my palm.

I was protected.

Right?

"Frank..." my voice was desperate. I wanted him to make the memories go away, make it like it was before, in blissful ignorance of the man who assaulted me.

Not a man, a demon.

Still, I couldn't get his eyes out of my mind—the dark pupils a slit of deep black against the bright yellow.

I could hear my heart pounding. When I finally spoke, my voice was an empty whisper. "It's real, isn't it?"

I looked everywhere but at him, letting my eyes travel around the room. What was I looking for exactly? An escape route? Maybe. As though escaping from this room, I would escape from the reality that was crashing down around me. Those weren't human eyes or human teeth. The way the shadows had moved around him as he closed in on me, the nightmarish imagery that blurred the lines of reality…

What was nightmare and what was real?

Because demons weren't real.

"This has to be some sort of joke," I said, sitting up. "I mean, these memories have been turned into bad dreams and distorted. How do I know I remember them correctly *now?*"

"Charlotte…" His eyes flitted to my chest as though he could feel the panic that was clamped around my heart. He clenched the bedsheet under his hand, and my eyes shifted to his fingers, knuckles turning white. When I raised my eyes to his, I saw the flash of yellow again, but this time it wasn't a trick of the light.

This time.

The conference.

It was real last time, wasn't it?

As I tried to get off the bed, Frank grabbed my wrist.

"Let me go," I said. My voice sounded on the verge of breaking, and his eyes softened as he watched me. I didn't want his sympathy, I just wanted him to let me go. I wasn't pulling against his grip, I was simply asking him.

I had to get out of here.

Let me go.

Please.

Frank

She asked me to let her go.

She asked me out loud, and she asked me with her eyes. You know, I had heard the saying *'a broken heart'* so many times. But the ache in my chest at the look in her eyes now, I got it. That pain she was feeling, that safe house she had built around herself, was coming crashing down, and it broke my heart.

Worse, it was my fault.

Without me, she could've lived without ever needing to have known.

I couldn't let her go.

Not now.

This wasn't just about her coming to terms with her past and what it meant for her future, this was about how I fit into that equation. Because somewhere along the line, things had changed between us, and I needed her.

Fuck.

I needed her.

Therefore, I needed her to understand.

I didn't let go of her wrist. "Let me explain."

"The nightmares started again only when I moved to the city, why?" she demanded.

"Larger demon population... the proximity would bring it out in you," I answered quickly.

She scoffed. "You just have an answer for everything, don't you?" Sitting on the edge of the bed in indecision, she still didn't fight my grip on her. But she wasn't coming closer to me either. The flashes of those nightmarish images still hung behind her eyes, and I could see it in every move she made.

"He could be here, couldn't he? My attacker?" Her voice was small, and the way she switched between anger, denial, passion, and sorrow was unsettling. I could see the struggle on her face, feel it in the way her heartbeat increased and then slowed before drumming again, in time with her thoughts as they traveled over the mountains of possibilities in her mind.

But I didn't answer her question, and her heart started pounding again. My fingers tightened around her wrist as the fight-or-flight reaction battled within her.

I didn't answer, not because I was holding something from her, but because the truth was, I didn't know. Her attacker could very well be residing in this city. I may have even taken him down during one of the arranged demon fights, and I wouldn't have known him from any other demon.

But that was before, and this was now.

That was before I had tasted the essence of the other demon's blood within Charlotte's, the way her sweet taste had been sullied and contaminated.

If I ever came across the demon who matched that scent, that taste, I wasn't sure even my advanced experience could protect the instinct that screamed at me internally to tear the other demon apart limb from limb and leave him to rot in pieces.

I eased my grip on her when she fell back against the pillows, but I couldn't help but notice she was closer to the edge of the mattress than she had been before. I hated to admit it hurt. Like she was playing nice, giving the illusion she had given in and accepted me and my truth, but was still plotting her escape. Her heart rate, the sweat on her neck, and her trembling lip, all these things betrayed her. She stared at the ceiling as my words sank in, and her mind reeled with her changing expressions as she struggled to work her way through this.

"If this is some sort of sick joke, Frank, I swear to God…"

"God can't help you now, but I can… if you let me."

Charlotte looked like she had been struck, and she clutched the necklace around her neck, willing it to protect her from whatever was clawing at the inside of her mind. "What did you mean the proximity would bring it out in me? Bring what out? What am I?"

"You're a woman, a human woman, who's been infected with demon blood. That night he started a process to make you his mate, but because he never finished it, you were left with it in your veins, struggling to contain it." I looked hard at her. "Your parents did the right thing by putting you in that school."

"It doesn't feel like it was the right thing."

I threw her a significant look. "Trust me, it was."

The demon wouldn't dare try to find her there— it would've no longer been worth the effort. The church and that school saved her the fate of being a slave.

I didn't think it would help to remind her of this right now.

"I don't feel like I've been struggling to contain anything, the necklace—"

"Is useless."

Charlotte clutched it protectively, her skin turning white where the points of the cross dug into her hand. "No. It's saving me."

I shook my head. "This isn't fiction, Charlotte. A necklace blessed by a priest or dipped in holy water does nothing. The only thing holding you back is you."

"I don't believe you. How do you even know these things?"

I hesitated. A hundred different scenarios of how she could react if I revealed the full truth flashed behind my eyes.

"I think you know the answer to that."

I could smell the fear in her sweat, and it was driving me crazy. I gritted my teeth, needing to keep myself under control while she worked through this.

For her.

She needed time, but time was apparently something I was running low on.

My demon was clawing to get out. The details of her full confession had driven it to the very surface of my skin, needing to claim her back, make her mine again.

These thoughts ran through the back of my mind and knotted together, combined with the pressing question, *how had I not sensed this earlier?*

If she had mentally linked that necklace to some

sort of control over what flowed through her blood, then she had damn good control over it. So strong was her belief in that piece of silver, she had controlled her internal conflict to a point I couldn't smell it on her.

Or maybe I had, and I just didn't recognize it for what it was.

Had she really gotten to me so much she had blurred the lines of my instinct? All that thought did was raise the realization that my attraction to her was so much more beyond the physical than I understood.

Or admitted.

I liked her, and I *cared* for her.

This was foreign territory to me and gave me something worth fighting for.

But also something to lose.

CHAPTER 22

Charlotte

My brows creased together as I stared at Frank. There was a nagging feeling in the back of my mind telling me the truth and to accept it—because what other explanation was there?

But I couldn't. Internally, I fought it.

But still.

How else could he know these things? Did he create this reality in his mind from things that he had seen and read?

I watched his face. His jaw was clenched again, the way he did when he was struggling to contain control. Previously, I had seen that look when he was trying to resist the urge to touch me, to take me, but now he was holding something else back. I looked at my hands, trembling slightly. When he grunted, my gaze was drawn back to him.

There was that flash of yellow again.

I think I know what he was trying to contain, but that was impossible.

It had to be.

That moment in the hotel after the conference when I had seen the color in his eyes, it wasn't a trick of the light, it was the one moment I had truly seen something beneath the surface. I often thought about his mask, the mask of the businessman that covered the playboy. But was it all just masks on top of masks? And beneath the surface was what?

If Frank were the same as my attacker, how could I trust him again? Was saying that all demons were identical the same as saying all humans are? Can there be good and bad demons or at least shades of gray?

"Doesn't God want you back where you belong?" I asked.

It was Frank's turn to scoff. "I doubt God would be bothered with us unlcss we regularly go around committing mass murder."

I made up my mind.

"Show me," I demanded.

"What?"

I gestured, indicating his body. "Show me."

He recoiled at my words, the hesitation heavy on his hunched shoulders.

"I don't think that's a good idea." Frank's voice was dark as he notably put distance between us.

"Please," I said. If I saw him, and he brought out the same fear in me that my attacker had, then I'd tell him to leave or leave myself. I could leave this apartment, my job, this city. I had done it before, and I could do it again. Because I didn't want to be afraid anymore, and if that meant I had to never see him again, so be it.

God, I made it sound so easy in my head.

But if he brought out something else in me—that something else I suspected we both knew was there, but I was still denying it, then at least he'd be here to help me deal with it.

Whatever *it* was.

The alternative—that nothing happened, and he was crazy or some obsessed occult fan—then I could move on knowing that none of this was real, and it would be just another chapter in my life I could close the book on. *The Frank Debacle* would reach legendary status amongst the girls in terms of batshit craziness, and then maybe years from now, we could laugh about it.

And maybe knowing he was crazy would make it easier to move on from him.

God, I hoped so.

Frank

Weighing my options, I sat up as my eyes took her

in. It didn't seem I had any choice left. I was at no risk of losing my cover by exposing my true self to her. Because really, who would believe her? But I *was* at risk of losing *her*, which was a high price to pay for the truth.

But she deserved to know.

Removing my shirt, I shrugged out of it and dropped the material off the side of the bed—no sense in shredding another piece of clothing. Besides, she'd get a better view this way.

Of the monster beneath.

Why was I shaking?

I kneeled in the middle of the mattress, facing her, and hesitating right up until the last moment, I started the physical release that would begin the change.

Charlotte watched wide-eyed as my muscles rippled, crawling beneath my skin in undulations of motion as my eyes turned yellow. The shadows moved around me, enclosing in on me, creating a cavern around us and blocking out the outside world.

I did this for no one else—*only her.*

As I allowed my inner demon to come to the surface, the skin on my face shifted with controlled movement, and I didn't take my eyes off hers. She stared into the yellow of my eyes with a slit of black for a pupil.

She shivered.

That hurt.

But she didn't look away and that gave me hope.

I saw it in her eyes the moment she accepted it.

It was real, it was all real.

I watched her process, my expression softening even as the black began to seep through my human skin like ink spilling from my veins and as I snarled through the pain of the transformation as my teeth sharpened further. Soon, my hair would disappear, and my skin would become the blackened ash it naturally is. Blackness broken only by red tattoo-like patterns that appeared like cracks across my body.

What would she see?

The truth of my being would be confronting for her, all yellow cat-like eyes and darkness and fire, and with skin blacker than the spaces between the stars, marked with the deep lines of demonic power.

I imagined it would be a lot to take in.

Would she still see Frank, or would she scream and run and be out of my life forever?

I felt like I had lost her already, and it hurt. It hurt more than I wanted to admit. As I stared into her widened eyes, her hands clasped over her mouth, and I growled again. Between the shadows was only us, and I was faced with the full weight of the realization that this might be it, that I may never have her again.

Just as it was bubbling below the surface, Charlotte saw the doubt in my eyes, the sorrow, and the humanity that peeked through the monster that was forming in front of her.

I saw her see it and saw the way her expression changed.

Whatever I was underneath, I was Frank.

Please, I begged internally, *don't forget who I am when you truly see me.*

The fear was gone from her as she watched me. Suddenly, she wasn't afraid of me, she was afraid *for* me. She didn't want me to suffer or hurt or to feel guilt for something that happened to her that I couldn't control. Because she knew, just as I did, that I'd spend the rest of my days protecting her.

Her control snapped.

CHAPTER
23

Frank

As she launched herself at me, I snapped back into the Frank she knew as I lost control of the change, and the process ended abruptly. The shadow around us cleared, the light blinding as reality pushed its way through the mask of darkness I had created around us. She pulled me toward her until our chests were pressed together and our tongues intertwined, hitching her skirt up so she could open her legs enough to straddle me.

My breathing became heavy. I was struggling now, really struggling to keep control.

I had been so close to unleashing my true self, something I hadn't done in many years. Now I wrestled to bring it back under control while her body heat infected me. I didn't want to hurt her, and my hands shook with the effort of holding her as she kissed me. Touching her wasn't a problem—I doubted it ever would be—but touching her gently was agony when my instinct was to throw her to the mattress, rip her skirt open, and take her while forcing her face into the pillow. Suddenly, her clothes were infuriating to me. The fabric was in the way of her bare back and breasts, a barrier to her heat as I sensed her getting wet. I growled, low and deep, a rumble that started in my chest and worked its way up through my throat as I buried my face in her neck.

"Take the necklace off," I mumbled against her skin.

"I'm scared to."

"Don't be, I'm here," I growled again, another deep quake from my throat that drew a shiver up her spine until she was trembling in my arms. I couldn't wait, she needed to learn. Ripping the necklace from her, I tossed it into the corner of the room as I bit into her shoulder. Charlotte arched into my touch, dragging her nails down my back. She could draw blood for all I cared. Her trembling intensified, and I knew she felt naked without the necklace. As though it was warming to her, she was so used to its touch that now she felt cold without it. She was truly exposed to me, but despite the prickling under her skin and the fight within her body, she held on. The control was up to her and had nothing to do with the necklace. It never had.

But she was desperately holding on to whatever control she could muster while at the same time coming undone under my fingertips.

Demon blood infected hers, and I hoped she was ready to know what that meant.

Either way, I was here to guide her.

I moved forward, laying Charlotte underneath me with one arm tucked around her waist, my other hand tearing at her blouse. The buttons protested as the fabric shred in my fingers and teeth as I literally tore her clothes off. If I destroyed the clothes, so be it, I'd buy her new ones. Because right now, those clothes were nothing more than obstacles to her body. I needed her soft skin under my fingers, touching, squeezing, spanking. I wanted to take her over and over again and needed it to last, but I also wanted to be rough, and if she let go with me, I just might be able to be as rough with her as I needed to bring myself back into line.

Throwing the ruined remains of her garment to the side, I mouthed at her breasts, my hands shaking as I undid the clasp on her bra and removed that barrier as well. As I ran my tongue over her nipple, it hardened in the heat of my mouth. She moaned, biting her bottom lip, and I frowned as I growled again.

She still wasn't letting go.

What did I have to do to make her?

My hips were bucking against her legs, and I was

erect and desperate to take her, to penetrate her and make her cry out my name.

I don't think I've ever needed release more than this.

Charlotte tilted her head back, pushing her breasts into my greedy mouth. When I glanced up at her face, her eyes were bright, watching me touch her, the heat coming off her skin in waves.

"Let go," I snarled.

"I can't," she whispered.

She was afraid. I could taste her fear through her sweat as I tongued her, running my mouth between her breasts to her other nipple. I could make it all better and give her the control over this part of her, the only part of her she'd always held back. I could teach her to control it rather than subdue it, use it when she wanted, and bring out the animal inside. I wouldn't take her like the other demon began to, and I'd never force her to be my mate.

If the priest hadn't sent her to the boarding school, it's likely the demon would've come back for her and finished the job, making her his.

The thought flared the rage inside me. The idea of Charlotte being nothing better than a sex slave fueled my anger.

If she were going to be a sex slave, she would be mine and mine alone.

I grunted and started yanking at her skirt, which Charlotte hastily removed after fumbling with the zipper, barely getting it open before I broke it. Tearing her panties from her body, the fabric ripped under my grip and elicited a yelp from her as it tugged roughly between her slit before coming free. When she was fully naked beneath me, I took control.

Because if she wouldn't let go of whatever she was holding back, I'd *make* her let go.

Then she could decide which path to take from there.

But first, this, because she wasn't the only one who needed it.

Pulling her upright by her arms, I threw her over my lap, gripping the fleshy orbs of her perfectly round ass and squeezing. I spanked her once with my palm. She cried out, and the sound echoed throughout the empty bedroom, bouncing off the floorboards and back to her, making her wetter than she already was.

I repeated the action on her other cheek, making her gasp as she kicked one leg out, pushing her knee against the mattress.

"Trying to get away from me?" I growled.

"Please..." she whimpered, and I spanked her again—once on each side—her cheeks starting to take on a pink hue.

"Please, *what,* pet?"

"More..."

The gravelly quality in her voice drew another

groan from me. She was intoxicating to me, so ready and willing to be taken it was both torture and ecstasy for me to draw it out. But this wasn't simply about taking her, it was about bending her will until she let go, then maybe she'd take me, finding control in the sweet freedom of release. I reached one hand in between her legs, she was so wet for me, so ready for me to fuck her. I slid one finger inside her, pumping it in and out a few times as she squirmed under my touch, trying to grind herself against my palm.

But she'd have to wait.

I removed my hand from her pussy, smirking at the frustrated sigh that escaped her lips. My cock twitched in my lap as I spanked her again and again, each time pausing to admire the color her skin was taking on, rubbing her ass in slow circles.

"Frank!" she cried out as I drove two fingers inside her waiting pussy, fucking her with my fingers and thumbing her clit. She moaned, making my shoulders and arms tense. The sound of her pleasure gutted me, and I constantly had to remind myself this was about *her* control, not mine. She clenched around my fingers.

I realized too late touching her like this was a mistake.

Once I felt inside her, felt her muscles move around my fingers, her warmth waiting to squeeze my cock with that delicious tight pussy, then heard that break in her voice as she cried out my name, my resolve to tease and torture snapped.

I couldn't wait any longer.

She wasn't the only one who was struggling to keep control.

I threw her off my lap, making her squeal as I sat next to her with my back against the headboard. Tugging my pants down over my hips as I moved, I kicked the tangle from my feet, pulling her roughly until she was straddling me.

"Ride me," I commanded, holding her legs as she hovered over me. When she smiled coyly at me, I snarled again. My eyes may have flashed yellow, I don't know, but this wasn't the time for her to test me. Yanking her down, I drove myself inside her with one deep thrust, her skin turning white under the tight grip of my fingertips.

Charlotte moaned with me as I was again fully sheathed inside her, her body stretching to accommodate me. As she began riding my cock, shifting her hips up and down, my length pulled in and out of her. But it still wasn't enough.

"Enough games." Sitting up straight, I wrapped my arms around her waist, pushing up into her and controlling her movements. Holding her still and thrusting into her, I used her body to pleasure me, drawing my release from the tightness of her around me. I pounded into her, hard and fast until a thin sheen of sweat covered my forehead and back. She cried out my name as I drove into her, gripping her ass with one hand, squeezing until she moaned again, finding that point between pleasure and pain.

"I love fucking your pussy, pet," I groaned out. "*Fuck.*" The last word nothing more than a breathy whisper as I buried my face into her hair, inhaling her scent.

Although she was moaning, those delicious sounds of pleasure tumbling from her perfect lips, she was still holding back. The necklace was gone, but she was keeping herself in check internally, holding onto that thread of control. I knew she could feel it, that tingle under her skin, the demon in her blood sensing mine, waiting to be unleashed. She had almost seen me, and I knew she had seen enough to be convinced that what I told her was real. I marveled at seeing her now, straddling me and riding my cock, her eyes heavy with lust when she looked at me, her lips parted, and her back arching into me.

She still wanted me, she *knew*, and she still wanted me.

And I wanted to help her.

I could feel it in her, as though the truth had only made her hold on tighter, desperately clutching at the illusion of control, kidding herself that one day the taint in her blood wouldn't break free. She'd never be wholly human again and would always

have that within her.
  I could help, but it was up to her.

CHAPTER 24

Charlotte

"Charlotte," Frank slowed his thrusts, moaning as I clenched around him. "I can give you control, let you take back what he did to you, but only if you want me."

"I've wanted you since the moment I saw you."

"More than sex, Charlotte. Although..." he held me while he thrust up into mc hard a few times, sighing at the sounds I made when he was rough with me. "I love being inside you." He touched my chin, waiting until my eyes opened from my blissful daze to look at him. "I mean, do you want me for me, knowing what you do, do you want to be with me?"

I breathed.

I didn't hesitate.

"Yes."

"Are you sure?"

Looking into his eyes, still bouncing on his lap and gripping his shoulders as the pleasure of our union bound us, I focused on him, on the sincerity in his face. He was worried about me. He was concerned that I was falling under his charms like all the other women, that I didn't understand everything now. Did he really think I couldn't feel it crawling under my skin, pumping through my blood? The closer I got to him, physically and emotionally, the harder it pushed against me from the inside, crying to be let out.

When he had started changing, and I had seen a glimpse of what he really was, I should've been afraid. Instead, what I felt was nothing short of lust. Pure stinging lust burst forth from me until I grabbed him before I was even aware my body had reacted.

This is the part that had frightened me, my body's reaction before my mind.

Pure instinct.

What scared me more was that I could tell myself it was just lust, but deep down, I knew that wasn't the right word starting with *L*.

I'd forged a connection with Frank through acceptance of the truth, giving in to it and all the possibilities it held. If this is who I was—this is a part of me living in my blood—then I could either embrace it or spend an entire lifetime fighting to keep it down.

Still, I held on to that thread of control, but I could feel it wavering.

I wasn't frightened of Frank but of myself and what would happen if I let go. Without knowing it, I had spent years of my life honing my ability to control this hidden side of me. What would happen when that changed?

He was still watching me, rocking inside me with torturously slow movements. This was more than sex, and it had been more from the very beginning and had grown into something I couldn't even describe. I didn't just want him, I *needed* him.

I needed all of him because he complemented all of me—the Yin to my Yang, the dark to my light.

The demon to mine.

"Frank…" He held my gaze, his eyes darting between my pupils, simultaneously desperate for the answer but afraid of what it might be. I was too.

I whispered, "I want you."

His eyes flashed the slightest hint of yellow beyond the deep brown of his irises, and he nodded. When he started to cut into his bicep with a fingernail, pressing hard to break through the tough skin, my eyes widened. "You don't have to."

"Don't be afraid. I want to." He showed no signs of pain or hesitation, and as the droplets of blood seeped from the wound, he held my eye contact. "Take it. Take me. Take back yourself. I won't force you, but if you want me, I'm yours."

Frank

Never would I coerce her. I didn't grab her head or neck and pull her to me. I wouldn't make her go near my blood with physical force, although we both knew I could. Maybe that's where the extra trust lay, in knowing I could hurt her, kill her in a moment, but I never would, and I'd take all the pain myself if it meant she was safe.

Continuing to rock within her, I watched her, enjoying the feel of her around me, gripping me as I claimed her and admired just how perfectly she fit around me. Charlotte bent her head and pressed her lips to my chest, and I tensed as she got close to the wound, slowing until I was barely moving inside her.

As she moved closer, I stilled. My instinct was to push into her, but I gritted my teeth against it. This needed to be her decision, her move—she needed to come to me.

When she kissed the wound, a whisper of a moan escaped my lips.

I tilted my head back, hyperaware of the seconds that passed when her lips hovered above my chest, her breath warm on the exposed blood. She leaned in, and when my blood met her lips as she parted them, darting her tongue over the cut, her pupils dilated before her eyes glowed yellow.

As she swallowed the blood, I felt it bubbling

within her veins, spreading throughout her and taking over. I was clutching the sheets, my arms shaking with the effort of staying still. Every fiber of my being was screaming at me to take control, to force the bond, to make her my mate.

The sight of my blood on her lip momentarily broke my control, and I pushed my chest out, forcing the wound toward her lips. Charlotte's head fell away from my chest, and a growl escaped her throat. She began to shiver violently, and when she screamed, she clenched around me.

"Charlotte..." I hovered my hands above her body, not sure what to do. Was this because I pushed her? Was this a normal reaction to a human bonding? "I'm sorry, I—" The breath was knocked from me as she pushed me flat on my back, slamming her palm into my chest.

Twisting to avoid hitting my head on the headboard, I adjusted my hips while still inside her. Charlotte's eyes glowed, and I didn't think I could find her more beautiful than I had before, but I was wrong.

She looked like she could take my life and steal my soul.

And I'd let her.

Lifting and dropping her hips with hard, heavy thrusts that had my fingers digging into the flesh of her thighs, she rode me. My head fell back into the pillows as she ground her hips into me, muttering obscenities as she moved as though possessed.

Perhaps she was.

We both were.

"Wait." I stilled, wanting her to take control, but part of that was maintaining enough of yourself to keep it slow. Charlotte had other ideas.

"No," she growled.

I sneered, opening my eyes to meet hers, yellow on yellow, as I felt her fingers snake around my neck.

"Do it." I dared her to go further, arching my neck and inviting her. She had already come so far. When her hand closed around my throat, she growled again, and I smirked. I wasn't afraid of her hurting me, she never could, but the delicious pressure on my neck escalated the pleasure of being inside her as she squeezed around my cock.

She leaned forward, gripping my neck as I pushed against her, arching into her touch, willing her to go further.

Grinning, I wasn't sure which Charlotte I liked more, the begging mess who was pining for my touch, or the animal Charlotte who was taking control. Guess I'd have to fuck her a lot more to decide.

"Mine," she whispered, her nails scratching against my skin as I embraced the pressure, tilting my chin up and offering myself to her.

Reveling in the feeling of her coming undone, of

her finally letting go of the part of her she had denied for so long, my pride was short-lived. The moment of satisfaction was destroyed by distraction as she pressed down onto me again, and I arched off the bed, groaning loudly. She was in control, she was in control of us both, and having her clench around me as she rode me was too much.

I wasn't going to last.

"Charlotte." It was almost a whimper, but I didn't have time to dwell on the humility of it. I wanted to gain back some control, but her hips moving against me was ecstasy, and I couldn't contain it. Bucking against her, her eyes were on mine, yellow on yellow. Digging my fingers into her hips, definitely leaving bruises on her pale skin, I cried out as I came, voice deep and otherworldly.

"Fuck!"

Charlotte

As I watched him come undone, a small chuckle escaped my lips before they curved into a mischievous smirk. He wanted me to let go, wanted me to take control, and the nail marks on his neck showed him what I could do.

As I felt the demon blood swirl in me, I knew I could do more. If I could channel this power, I could do so much more.

But the smile was soon wiped from my face as he sat up, his hand at my throat, applying the pressure I hadn't dared to.

He grinned, exposing those sharp teeth as I squeaked.

"You didn't think you were done that easily, did you?"

I felt him twitch inside me, still hard despite his orgasm, and I squeaked again, unable to say much with the pressure he was applying to my throat. When he started to move inside me, still fully hard, my eyes widened.

Even when I was in control, I wasn't really.

Frank owned me, he knew it, and now I knew it too.

He licked a droplet of dried blood off my lip before pushing his tongue into my mouth, not letting up on the pressure on my neck. I groaned against his mouth, the yellow in my eyes flaring again at the tiniest taste of the remnant of his blood. I could feel it, my eyes changing, like a rush of light passing over my eyes before my vision cleared, and I could see the world with clarity I hadn't seen before.

Frank used the leverage on my neck to lift me off him, his grin spreading as I whimpered when I lost the feeling of fullness as his cock slid out of me.

"Bend the fuck over."

My back arched at his command. "Frank—"

He gripped my neck, cutting my words off. "Bend over." His voice was dark, controlled, promising punishment. "I won't ask again."

I nodded against his hand, testing him by pulling away, and when he released my neck, I moved and kneeled, bending over and arching my back, pushing my ass out in a tease.

The way he spanked me as he moved, I realized I might regret that tease.

I looked back at him as he rolled off the bed and stood by the edge of the mattress, admiring my form.

"You're far from innocent, looking over your shoulder at me like that." I didn't know what to say, my mind was a fog, so I said nothing. "Come here," he commanded, and I backed up toward him, and he hummed his approval. "That's right, bring that ass over here."

When I was at the edge of the bed, he spanked me hard with his flat palm, laughing when my immediate response was to growl at him. He did it again, and the growl in my throat turned into a snarl. A gut reaction, but I didn't fight it.

"What are you going to do about it?" he teased, palming his cock and rubbing it between my pussy lips and over my clit, making me jump. I moaned as he pushed the tip of his cock inside me, just the tip, smirking as I ground against him. When I'd try to push back toward him, he'd spank me again, moving just the head of his cock as he teased it in and out of my eager pussy. Just the head, so I would be forced to stretch around him, again and again, before he'd pull out.

"Frank, *please.*" This wasn't the breathy whisper he was used to, not the begging he had enjoyed from me before. This was a frustrated snarl between clenched teeth.

He grabbed his cock, rubbing it up my pussy and kept going until he was pressing it against the puckered entrance to my ass. I gasped, "Frank!"

"Charlotte?" he whispered. I hummed, but my voice was full of distraction as he was applying pressure against my ass, moving his hips gently, increasing the pressure with each forward push. Every tease sent a shiver up my spine until I was trembling under his touch and the promise of the invasion.

"May I?" he crooned.

"Frank, I've never..."

"I know." He continued pushing forward but never breaking through, waiting for my okay. "I won't put it all the way in, not this time. I just want to feel you." His voice was gentle and kind but hadn't lost that commanding edge from only moments before.

Biting my lip, I could still feel the fight going on internally, and I wanted him to claim me in every way, to take all of me.

Hoping I wouldn't regret this decision, I said, "Be gentle."

Frank groaned as he pushed forward again, breaking through the resistance of my body. I cried out as he penetrated my ass, the head of his cock stretching me open while he was still wet from my pussy.

"Fuck." Frank gritted his teeth. "I'm not going to last long if you're going to grip me like that."

I just nodded, concentrating on relaxing my body to the intrusion. I'd be lying if I said there wasn't some pain, but it was more of a pressure. The stretch was unlike anything I felt before, and I realized he had said he wasn't going all the way in.

If this is what it felt like with him only in a little bit...

Squirming, I adjusted to the feel of him. His breathing was labored behind me, and when I did an experimental clench around him, I grinned when he groaned and gripped my hips.

When he leaned forward, I cried out as he was pushed inside me that little bit further. He mumbled an apology and stilled, reaching his arm around my body and finding my clit. He stayed still inside me, twitching at the grip of my virgin passage around his cock as he rubbed my clit. When I moaned, he increased the pressure of his fingers, whispering in my ear about how tight I was and how hard I made him. I felt myself relax around the intrusion as the wetness from my pussy dripped over his fingers.

"I barely even have to move, you're so tight," he whispered as he rubbed my clit in small circles. "I'm so sensitive from fucking your pussy." He pushed forward again, sinking his cock inside me another inch as I cried out again. "Let me. Just a little."

His breathing became ragged as he rubbed me, feeling me relaxing against the intrusion. My leg twitched as he pushed inside me, pulling out slowly before doing it again. He said he wasn't even halfway inside me, but it was enough, more than enough to bring him off. He needed me to come and wanted to bring me the same pleasure he was feeling.

Because next time he was inside my ass, he might not be able to hold back.

I couldn't respond to any of this because I couldn't find the words. The pleasure that was building was unlike anything I had experienced before.

"Come for me, pet," Frank said. I moaned again as he began fucking me a little bit faster with small movements in and out, keeping as much control of the motion as he could. "You're opening up to me," he growled. "You're such a good pet."

His words were enough to send me over the edge, his voice intoxicating in the best way, and with the pressure on my clit, I came. My eyes widened as I cried out, tightening around him. He pushed in a little more, my body clenching and fighting the intrusion as I rode out the waves of my orgasm, more intense as he kept rubbing my clit, drawing out my pleasure. He continued the small, measured movements in and out of me, and just as I was flittering on the last wave of my high, he groaned, loud, coming inside me while I twitched under him, gripping and releasing him involuntarily.

"Fuck!" he roared, gritting his teeth as he pumped into me.

I squeaked when he shifted, and he paused, gauging my reaction before slowly pulling out of me while his arm twitched as he gripped my hip. His head dropped to his chest, his breathing labored.

"Fuck," he repeated as he rubbed my ass gently. "Are you okay?"

"Yes," I said before sighing and rolling onto my side, my legs cramped from the intensity of my orgasm. Frank stood still for a moment, pulling air into his lungs to clear his head. Padding across the bedroom to the ensuite, he returned with a damp washcloth and gently cleaned me up. I chuckled when his display of affection ended there, and he tossed the cloth back into the bathroom from where he stood before collapsing heavily next to me.

Rolling over, he pulled me to him, my back to his chest, and rested his chin on my shoulder as his arms wrapped around my stomach.

"You sure you're okay?"

"That was intense, Frank."

"Are you sore?"

"A little." When he tensed behind me, I added, "But only a little."

Frank trailed his hand down and over my ass. "We can go again if you want."

I smirked. "Not tonight."

"Oh good, so it's not off the table for another night."

Laughing quietly, exhaustion was taking over. "Go to sleep, Frank."

He sat up just enough to grab the corner of the duvet from the end of the bed and pulled it over us, tucking it around my shoulders.

Grinning into the pillow, I reminded myself to tease him for being a big softie later. Pulling me tight against his body, I stared ahead when I sensed the tenseness of his muscles—it felt like he was hesitating. Then he moved, kissing me on the cheek, letting his lips linger over my ears with words unsaid before lying down again.

I smiled as I curled into him, thinking, *I love you too.*

CHAPTER 25

Charlotte

Staring at the clock on the bedside table, I watched as it slowly clicked over the minutes until the early morning. Frank was still behind me, his chest pushed into my back, and his arm draped lazily around me, brushing the underside of my breasts. I was sure he was still awake, his breathing against my neck too uneven, hitching and releasing with his thoughts.

"Frank?"

He mumbled an acknowledgment, still relaxed from his orgasms. "Are you okay?" he muttered, his hand automatically moving to the smooth cheek of my ass. After unleashing whatever was pent up inside me after the way I took him, my hands around his neck, *he* was worried about having hurt *me*.

It's okay, I won't tell anyone your secret, that you're a big softie.

My grin faded. That wasn't what was on my mind.

"What have we started?" I whispered, running my tongue over the inside of my mouth, remembering the metallic taste of his blood on my lips.

He shifted in response to me, drawing me closer to him, and I moved against him, reliving the moment of our bonding. He felt so good against me, and I closed my eyes for a moment, taking in the feel of his skin on mine. I felt soft and delicate next to him, a masculine case containing immeasurable power. Frank rolled onto his back and pulled me with him until I was curled up against him and my head rested in the crook of his shoulder.

It was comfortable there.

"We started the mating process," he finally answered.

"What does that mean?"

"Bonding together for life. Our lifespans are longer than yours, and if we are to bond with a human, we give them our blood."

"We're not bonded together already?"

"In a way." He smiled, briefly. "But you need to drink my blood again." In answer to my questioning look, he added, "Only once more."

I let his words wash over me, *only once more*, and

then what? Would I still have control over my life? Frank being my boss, *inside the bedroom and out*, as he had said, while fun, I wasn't sure if I could accept the reality of him being in complete control of everything about me. If that even was the case.

I wanted to be with him, I really did. I wanted to have him near me, around me, inside me, every minute of every day. I wanted to be *his* but wanted him to *mine* on the same level—a partnership, equals. Could I ever be equal with one who wasn't human?

Would I even still be human?

I swallowed. "If we finish bonding, what will I become?"

Frank squeezed me against his side, a growl emanating low in his throat. He replied sleepily, "Mine."

When I woke to Frank dressing with haste, I felt the frown immediately on my face. Surely, he wasn't sneaking out after everything we had been through. I glanced at the window, and no sunlight was creeping around the heavy curtains yet, so it was still dark outside.

It was the middle of the night, and he was dressing in silence.

I forced myself to think straight and asked, "Is everything okay?"

"No." He didn't even pause in his movements when he looked at me, his expression was stern, something I hadn't seen on him before. It didn't suit him. "I need to go help Mike." He shrugged on his shirt. "I'm sorry, it's an emergency."

"What's happened? Can I help?"

Frank stared at me as I sat up in bed dragging the sheet with me—it smelled like him. "Maybe you can. Get dressed, quickly."

I dressed in jeans and a t-shirt and grabbed my essentials, following Frank out of the apartment and locking the door behind me as I was still zipping up my jacket.

The chill from the night air affronted us as we reached the basement, and I had to jog to keep up with Frank's long strides. Climbing into his car, I barely had the door closed before he took off, pulling out of the parking garage and onto the street, causing other vehicles to brake and horn their discontent. I instinctively grabbed the seat, my legs squeezed together, and the leather protested under the grip of my fingertips.

As we left the city, I glanced at Frank, the uncertainty plastered across his face, and I couldn't wait any longer to ask.

"What's happened?"

"Mike's a demon too."

"What?" I spluttered. "Is the whole damn company full of demons?"

Frank smirked despite his obvious concern. "No, just me and him."

"Wait." I glared at him, images running through my mind of sketches—an artist's interpretations of a place I'd rather not imagine. I asked, "Your designs, did they come from..." trailing off, Frank didn't say anything, only threw me a significant look. I didn't pry further, preferring to leave that line of questioning in the back of my mind to be dealt with later.

"So, Mike's in trouble?" I prompted when silence filled the car again.

Frank sighed heavily, running a hand down his face, briefly plastering the dark curls to his forehead. "Demons have certain urges, sex obviously, but also a violent streak. I contain mine by fighting with other demons." He looked sideways at me as though waiting for a negative reaction, but I just continued to stare at him.

"It's arranged fighting," he explained. I didn't ask for an explanation, but apparently, he wanted to offer me one. "Everyone is there because they want to be, no one is forced to fight. Mike, he refuses to find an outlet for his urges. He seems to think he can contain them through willpower alone. Last night he went out, somehow ended up in a drug lab belonging to a gang, and…"

"And?"

"He may have killed some people."

"Jesus, Frank, why the hell did you bring me?"

"We've started a bonding. I thought your presence might help him calm down. Ground him, show him there are other ways and that a future on Earth is possible. Show him that he has support here." His eyes squeezed shut for a brief moment, and he shook his head as though he was scolding himself for having such an empathic thought.

A future on Earth is possible.

I watched him but said nothing further, and we drove the remainder of the way in silence. What was there that could be said?

Two hours out of the city limits, and I had watched as the high-rises turned into suburban homes and then into long stretches of fields. Pockets of small towns dotted the dark highway before even those weren't there anymore. The streetlights were few and far between until there were none at all, and everything beyond the scope of the headlights was pitch black.

Frank didn't slow down.

Apparently, his night vision was better than mine.

Trying to concentrate, I considered what exactly it was I was supposed to do to calm Mike. I hadn't had much to do with him since I started my job. Mike had his own personal assistant, Lainie, who I had met only a handful of times as Frank and Mike looked after different spectrums of the business. Would some demon instinct kick in for me so I could help? Was I supposed to be tough or nurturing, pushy or understanding? I kept glancing at Frank as we drove, every second that passed filling me with a doubt I hadn't entertained while we were in the bedroom together.

This was a life full of things I didn't know how to handle.

CHAPTER
26

Charlotte

The sun was making its way over the horizon, an angry orange glow that shimmered in the distance as Frank pulled off the road onto a dirt track. I gripped the door handle as the car started to rattle as Frank drove it across the rocks and potholes. He barely slowed down when the terrain changed, and I was both touched and floored by his disregard for the state of the expensive vehicle. Was this born from an abundance of funds or concern for his friend? Maybe both.

Parking in a small clearing, Frank indicated for me to get out of the car, pressing a finger to his lips as I undid my seat belt. The beeping sound the car made as I opened the door seemed louder than possible in the empty woods, and the insects paused in their songs at the intrusion of sound.

Frank turned off the headlights.

I had thrown on the first pair of shoes I'd found near the bed—a pair of heeled boots—and struggled to keep my balance across the uneven ground. Frank came up silently next to me, pocketing his keys and steadying my elbow with his other hand. As we approached the building, we passed through piles of rubbish—buckets and hoses, discarded and broken lab equipment stained a dark brown from cooking up something sinister. The front door was partially open, uninviting to the black hole beyond. I could smell the chemicals, heavy in the air around the house, a sickly carbon scent that burned the inside of my nostrils as I breathed in. Scrunching my face in distaste, I didn't need to know the ins and outs to guess the scale of the drug manufacturing being done here.

Frank held an arm out in front of me as he looked past the front door before pushing it open fully to allow what little light was outside to seep in. Tiny illuminations of various indicators were dotted around the room, and the open door created more shadows than pockets of light. My skin prickled uncomfortably, every shadow potentially hiding threats from me.

Frank made his way through the room, holding his arm out so I couldn't move ahead of him as if I'd be tempted to in the first place. We moved silently down the hallway, every creak of the floorboards breaking the emptiness as we followed the only light source in the house, the only light left on. As we neared the rear of the building, I smelled something else, something worse, something sharp and metallic that had me baring my teeth in response.

Blood.

We came into the back room, and I clapped a hand over my mouth when I took in the scene around me.

Mike was standing in the middle of the room, his fists clenched and his body heaving with every breath. How long had he been standing there? It had taken us hours to get to him.

His eyes were bright yellow, staring at the wall behind Frank as though he could see a masterpiece worth viewing. His shirt was stained with violent blood splatters across the white fabric, and the consequences of his actions were strewn across the floor around him. Decapitated, mangled bodies of those who had been in the wrong place at the wrong time. Or did he seek them out?

Taking in the chains hanging from the ceiling and the photos tacked directly into the walls of the women who had been unfortunate enough to be in them, fear visible in their eyes even from the Polaroids, I found any sympathy I had for the dead men failing.

Mike's thin pupils slowly shifted from the wall to

Frank's face, his head following the movement of his eyes moments later. The effect was mechanical and unsettling, his neck twisting and his eyes flashing as he sniffed the air.

Frank's brow furrowed as he glanced back at me, his eyes widening and opening his mouth to speak.

But Mike had already moved.

Mike was on me, pinning me against the wall and grunting against my neck as he tried to restrain my struggling hands. I barely had time to react. He was standing in the middle of the room, and I was trying to keep the contents of my stomach where they were. Then, he was in front of me, grabbing my wrists before I had even started trying to pull away.

He was running on pure instinct, an animal that had picked up the scent of another dominant male in its territory. When I opened my mouth to scream, a hand was clamped roughly over my face as he ground himself against me. Frank roared and grabbed the back of Mike's shirt, launching him off me and propelling him across the room. As Mike's body hit the wall opposite, he was on his feet before the wall had finished crumbling away from the impact. His hands clenched and relaxed as he began pacing back and forth in a short line. He was shooting Frank looks of distrust and hate intermittently while staring at me. I could almost hear the blood pulsing through him.

Perhaps I could.

"Mine," Frank growled at him.

Mike snarled, and I recoiled at the inhuman sound, his face distorting with rage as the lines of red and black peaked through his skin before the sound faded into a hiss. Frank stood in front of me, blocking me from Mike's view. "If you need to get this out of your system, fight me."

"Let me have her," Mike snapped. His eyes flickered to Frank for only a moment before settling on me again. He sniffed the air around us, ending with a deep breath that made my skin crawl. "You can finish your bond after. I need her only for a couple of hours, maybe a night."

"Back the fuck up, Mike. I don't want to have to hurt you." Frank was holding his hand out as though trying to tame a lion in a circus.

Mike's eyes cleared just enough for him to shake his head, "Don't want to kill you," he growled again, a sound that reverberated deep in his throat, as though talking was an effort he could barely sustain. "Give me the woman. I won't kill her." He craned his neck to look over Frank's shoulder and licked his lips.

My stomach twisted as I felt my body respond to the way Mike was looking at me, wanting to devour me. I couldn't help it. It was impulse, instinct, every nerve in my mind told me not to react, but it happened anyway. When I rubbed my legs together, Mike's lips curled, and he made an obscene gesture with his tongue.

Frank sniffed the air and cast an angry glance at me, growling again when he turned back to Mike, his voice a thunderous threat. "Fight me, for if you touch her, I *will* kill you."

As Mike approached Frank, I backed up against the wall. If he came for me again, I wouldn't be fast enough to get out of there. I trusted Frank to protect me, but whatever I was supposed to be doing here was obviously *not* working.

Frank shook his head, throwing Mike a dirty look and moving in front of him again as he tried to skirt around him to get to me. "You fucking idiot. I warned you what would happen if you didn't find an outlet."

There were moments of recognition passing across Mike's eyes, and with each step he took toward Frank, his neck would twitch, twisting his head to the side in jerking motions, a physical manifestation as he fought for control.

"Charlotte." Frank didn't bother to lower his voice. Anything he said would be picked up by Mike's heightened senses anyway. "Get out. Find a room and lock yourself in." He shushed me angrily as I went to interrupt. "Don't come out until I say so. *Only* if *I* say so."

Nodding, I followed Frank's instructions, hastily leaving the room. It took a grand effort to ignore my instinct to go back and protect him while the snarling behind me doubled as the men—demons— launched at each other. Putting one foot in front of the other, I forced myself down the hall as I heard furniture breaking as someone, hopefully not Frank, was thrown through something. I clamped a hand over my mouth when I squeaked as the house rattled. Did one of them just get thrown through a wall? Hesitating for a moment, I turned abruptly and locked myself in a small room.

I wanted to turn on the light, but if I were supposed to be hiding, that would just give away my location. So, I waited in the dark in a stranger's room, unable to move around for fear of making too much noise. My nostrils flared as I smelled the changes in the air from their fight, smelling like danger, power, blood, and dominance.

And there was nothing I could do to help.

CHAPTER 27

Charlotte

Not sure how long I waited in that room when I heard the sounds moving down the hallway. I carefully shrank further into the shadows, holding my breath. The sound shifted past the door and continued out the front of the house.

It didn't sound like fighting anymore.

Someone was being dragged.

I found myself praying that Frank was safe. The irony of praying for the safety of a demon not lost on me, but I prayed anyway. A small internal monologue, wishing him safety and that Mike can be helped.

God, don't judge me for wanting to help him.

For wanting him.

My knuckles whitened as I gripped my hands together under my chin, *old habits die hard,* as I pressed my lips together. It struck me that after all these years of pushing Him aside, it seems God had found his way back into my life at the same time I had found Frank.

Or he had found me.

"Charlotte."

Frank's voice sounded from outside the door. I moved to unlock it, my hand hovering over the brass for a split second before I pressed the lock and turned the knob.

"Oh, Frank." I sighed. His clothes were shredded and splattered with blood patterns to match Mike's, although not quite as violent, a large stain from a wound where the blood had seeped into the fabric, already drying around the circle of red. The cut he had made on his chest earlier that night when we were alone had been torn open and joined by more cuts as though a wild animal had attacked him.

"I'm fine." He grabbed my arm and led me down the hallway, and I was thankful to note we were leaving. "It's not all my blood."

As he opened the car door and pushed me in, cradling my head in his palm, I asked, "Mike?"

Frank's lip curled. "He's in the trunk," he said, kicking the back of the car as he walked around it. Whether the expression was pride or disdain, or maybe a bit of both, I couldn't tell. He slid into the driver's seat, stretching his fingers out and cracking his knuckles. I winced at the sound, too many cracks for the number of joints he should have.

When he looked at me, I said, "Your face."

"What about my face?"

Reaching out tentatively, I touched his cheek. "Aside from a nasty cut, you might have a black eye."

"Shit." He started the car. "Not the fucking face, Mike," he mumbled as he reversed the car, noisily skidding on the rocks as he turned out.

Frank

As we drove—considerably slower than we had on the way in, mind you—I didn't see the point in attracting unwanted attention, especially because of our passenger in the trunk. Charlotte jumped every time there was a thump from inside the trunk.

"Is he going to be okay?" she whispered.

"He'll be fine. Maybe now he'll listen to me and find an outlet."

"Those men?"

I shrugged. "Police will find them eventually."

"But..." Charlotte looked panicked. "Our fingerprints?"

"The only thing you touched was the door handle, and I wiped it."

"What about you?"

I just smiled. "Our blood is all over that place, Charlotte. I'm not worried about fingerprints." When I looked at her and saw the worry on her face, I continued, "Neither our blood nor our prints will do them any good."

We drove in silence for a while, Charlotte watching the shadows of the trees moving past the window before eventually the small towns dotted throughout the area increased in number. When we could see the glow from the city in the distance, she spoke again, "Frank?" she said and I hummed my acknowledgment and waited for the line of questioning I knew would come eventually. "If I want to go to church, will I burn?"

My laugh was loud and bark-like, then I cleared my throat, trying to cover it unsuccessfully when I saw the look on her face. "This isn't the movies, Charlotte, you won't burn. You can go to church."

She looked out the window again. I could almost feel the questions stirring inside her but didn't want to push her. This was something she needed to do in her own time. I still harbored fear that in the end, she'd reject me. We hadn't gone past the point of no return yet. Although, if she left it now, every demon she encountered would be able to smell both me and the other demon on her. The males would try to take her, try to dominate and claim her like Mike had, and the females would try to kill her. I pressed my lips together. If she were going to leave me, she'd need to be taught how to defend herself and kill demons if necessary.

I made a face, thinking that would be a fun conversation to have. True death for us meant either full dismemberment or removal and burning of the heart.

Or both if you wanted to be safe.

Charlotte watched me, and my face shifted as I worked through my thought process. I wished she'd talk to me. I could almost feel all the questions bundled up inside her. She just needed to find a loose thread and start pulling, and everything else would follow.

I wanted to push her, but I had already done that enough. She needed to step up.

Finally, I relented and spoke first. "Ask me all the questions you need, Charlotte," I instructed.

She closed her eyes and sighed. "I have so many, I don't know where to start."

"It doesn't matter where you start. I'll always answer you honestly."

"How is what we have different from the other demon who made me drink his blood?"

My hands gripped the steering wheel. The reminder that another demon had touched her flared inside me, and I felt myself getting hard in response. My body was telling me to pull over and take her on the side of the road, even better that Mike was in the trunk, to show him that she belonged to me and me alone. I could press her face into the back seat, make her cry out my name, and make sure that Mike and any other demon knew she was mine.

Releasing a slow breath, I knew the question came from innocence and not understanding, but it still cut deep to be compared to a demon who entrapped and forcibly took young girls. I took another deep breath and let it out.

"You were still a child, and bonding with a child makes them no better than a slave to you for the duration of their lives. He forced you. A true bonding is done between adults, willingly, which is why I wanted you to come to me. It had to be your choice." I looked at her. She was so beautiful, the light passing across her face with every streetlamp we drove under. Her eyes were wide as she took in everything I said, her lips slightly parted in thought. I stared at the road again, trying not to get distracted by thoughts of putting something between those waiting lips of hers.

I could tell she was working on absorbing this information without judgment, and I wasn't keen to consider how she would cope when the shock wore off. She was strong, but an acknowledgment of supernatural beings was a lot to take in.

"If we finish the bonding..." I paused then continued, "... you will not be my slave. You will be you, but you'll be mine too, and I'll be yours. A bonding can be broken, but it's a long and painful process. Bonding is creating a partnership, and there's really no better word for it than a bond."

"Do demons bond with other demons?"

"Of course."

She fell into silence, and this time I let her keep her silence until she was ready with the next question.

Charlotte

It seemed impossible to imagine the demons I had pictured as a child in church bonding for life, essentially getting married but on a much more instinctual level. The demons I thought of brought pain and suffering and tortured those who sinned in their lives on Earth. If those demons had lives of their own, dreams and wants, then angels must too. Did they also come to Earth when they felt they couldn't find what they needed at home? Were there angels here too? I couldn't imagine heaven not providing all the things that one could want and need.

"Have you ever bonded before?"

I saw the smile on his lips before I had finished asking the question. Really, his reputation should've been enough to answer it for me, his behavior hadn't exactly alluded to a man who was into monogamy. But for some reason, I needed to hear it from him. The smirk he had told me he was mentally running through all the beings—humans and demons alike—he had bedded.

"No," he said finally.

I nodded, happy to be his first but also weighed down with the responsibility of seeing this through. He said I needed to come to him willingly, but could I willingly leave him knowing what I knew? He threw me a glance, the contentment sliding from his face.

Sometimes, I'm sure he could read my thoughts.

"Don't come to me out of pity, Charlotte. The bonding must be through *desire* to create a bond." His following smile was empty. "I'm a big boy. I can handle rejection if this isn't for you."

I turned away, looking out the window again, gazing at a world that only a day ago had made so much more sense.

I wanted Frank, but did I really want everything that came with him?

CHAPTER
28

Frank

Returning to work as though everything was normal was, if possible, even more difficult now than it had been before.

Awkward was not something I normally considered—it was never a problem. But that was before I cared about the damn human who was in my life.

Being in the office after *almost* having sex had been irritating. Being in the office after having sex and then fighting had been infuriating. But being in the office after starting the process of creating a human slash demon bond with a co-worker and then seeing your boss's partner murder victims...

Now, *that* was awkward.

Charlotte's work began to suffer, her mind constantly elsewhere, the memories of the attack from her childhood mingled with the sensations of the bond of my blood coursing through her veins. I was over her, all around her, as she was me. The scent and feel of her was completely embedded in my mind.

If this is what it was like for me, I can accept that for her, it was another level of complicated.

Staring at the computer screen, she didn't seem to be able to concentrate on anything, and she'd go minutes without typing. I'd watch her out-of-focus figure in my peripheral vision, sitting at her desk, staring.

Struggling.

Obviously, I noticed her struggle. I'm not a complete moron. When she smiled, it was empty, and I could see in her eyes that she *wanted* to feel the happiness behind the expression but simply couldn't. The decline in the quality of her work didn't bother me, but the fact this situation was troubling her so much she was losing the control she normally maintained over herself did.

All shit hit the fan when *Damien* came into the office again.

Grinning, I thought about the nickname Charlotte had given him. She had referred to him by this nickname once in conversation, resulting in utter confusion from me, followed by a hearty laugh at her explanation.

His name was Peter, at least that was the name

he went by on Earth, not that it mattered.

I watched as Peter strolled past Charlotte's desk as he had a handful of times since their first encounter. I had not yet told Charlotte what these uninvited guests came in to see me for, and I hadn't planned to. But things had changed between us, and I felt she was owed honesty about all parts of my life, especially if she were to be a bigger part of it.

Long story short, they were after money.

I had managed to get them to come to me and not Mike, so I at least had some level of control over the situation. Mike would be too lenient, as it was easier to give in than fight them about it. Mike had been quite subdued after I had pulled him from my car trunk by his collar, bringing his face close to mine to check his eyes and releasing him when I confirmed they were back to the human gray. Mike had agreed—begrudgingly—to attend the fight clubs on a semi-regular basis before slapping me on the back and murmuring a congratulations on the bonding process. He had stumbled into his apartment building and slammed the door without looking back.

Sighing, I stood and rolled my shirt sleeves up, walking around the front of my desk and leaning against it, waiting for my uninvited guest to come to me.

While Charlotte had previously been staring blankly at her screen, now her shoulders were tense, and she was staring with so much additional intensity, it was obvious she was trying hard not to look at Peter. So I wanted this over with quickly.

This monogamy thing was so complicated. I had spent so long with no one to consider but myself and Mike.

But now…

… this was going to take some getting used to.

But then, I'd look at her. She'd be sitting at her desk with her brow furrowed, looking at the computer screen without really seeing it, and I found it sexy as hell. I grinned. She was more than just sexy, she was desirable and truly beautiful.

I wondered how she'd take to finding out other demons were bribing me to keep my true identity a secret.

The downfall of creating an empire was that I had a lot to lose if I were made to go back underground.

Literally.

I kept my face impassive as Peter came into my office with his hands shoved in his pockets and his shoulders slumped forward, but a devious grin plastered on his pale face.

"What now, Peter?" I drawled. "Are you going to throw burning holy oil at me? Finish crafting your demon blade? Pack a shotgun with salt?"

Peter snickered. "They're all such good ideas. I do like to keep my options open."

"How much do you need this time?"

"I smelled you on her."

When my back stiffened, Peter's sneer widened to display his sharp teeth, large canines, perfect for ripping out jugulars.

"Tell me what you want and then leave," I said through gritted teeth.

Peter laughed as my arm twitched, stretching the fabric of my shirt as my muscles tensed. "She smells good, but she's not quite yours yet, is she? I could still take some."

My teeth were bared, and a snarl was past my lips when Peter's head was yanked backward, bending his spine on a sharp curve. Charlotte's lips were at his ear, her fingers tangled in his hair as she twisted, pulling him back further. He growled at her, and when she bared her teeth, the yellow passed across her eyes.

"What's the matter? I thought you wanted me?"

My jaw dropped as she tugged Peter's hair again, forcing him off his feet when his back wouldn't bend at the angle required to stay standing. When he started to get up, she kneed him in the face, dropping her elbow on the back of his head, knocking him to the floor again.

"You little bitch," he hissed, standing and holding his hands out to grab her throat. A move he didn't get to finish as my arm wrapped around his neck in a chokehold, crushing him against my chest. Peter turned his head as much as the hold would allow, his eyes turning a deep yellow as he looked at me. "I'll make you regret this."

I scoffed. "You need me more than I need you." I released Peter. "I'll transfer you some money, but I better not see you again for a *long* time."

Watching him leave, I turned to Charlotte. She was staring at her hands, her breathing heavy and uneven.

"Thank you," I said. "But I had it under control."

"I could see you were getting angry." She paused, correcting herself. "I could *feel* it."

"Where did that come from?" I asked.

"What?"

"Those moves."

Charlotte turned, looking at the empty hallway, Peter long gone from the office. "Basic self-defense moves, you know? I did a class with Meredith when I moved to the city. *Big city moves for a big city girl,* she had said." Charlotte frowned at me. "How long has this been going on? I've seen all the accounts, so how are you hiding this?"

My smile was hollow. "I don't use the business accounts." Trying to keep the offense from my voice, Charlotte looked at the floor, flushing and twisting her hands together. She was trying not to judge as I had judged myself many times before.

Could a demon even be judged by human standards and vice versa? A man can be proud and defensive if his honor is questioned, but can a demon?

Apparently, we could.

I continued, "I use my own money, Charlotte."

"How long has this been going on?"

"For as long as I could afford it. They want the luxury, the freedom, but they don't want the work."

Discomfort crossed her face. "But, you're a demon right? Can't you just... kill him?"

"We still have rules, Charlotte. I wouldn't last long on Earth if I went around killing everyone who bothered me, demon or otherwise."

She nodded, looking around behind her again at the empty hallway. I watched her. She was glancing back at her hands, then around my office, at everywhere but directly at me. Once the question about the business side of things had been asked, that professional part of her faded, and she was lost in her thoughts again.

"What's wrong?" I asked, breaking the silence I could no longer stand. My patience for giving her the time she needed was wearing thin, no matter how I tried to hide it. My desires for her had only increased with time, and the longer she made me wait to touch her, the harder it was.

"Something wasn't right."

"Tell me."

"When I was attacking Damien, I wanted to hurt him." When I opened my mouth to speak, she held up her hand. "No, Frank, I mean I *really* wanted to hurt him." When she finally met my eyes, hers were wide and frightened. "I wanted to make him bleed, make him suffer, to really *feel* his pain. I wanted his blood…"

"Charlotte…"

"What am I? Am I a monster now?"

"Am I?"

"Frank…" But she had hesitated, and in not answering, she had already told me everything I needed to know. I wanted her to make this choice herself, to come to me of her own free will, no tricks, or not at all. She had felt the desire surging through her veins, the lust for violence, for blood, and it scared her. It challenged the fragile hold on control of her life she thought she had.

How could I make her understand that she had control, and all she needed to do was learn it? I could help her. But I knew her well enough to know that if I pushed too hard, tried to take over and teach her the control she needed, she'd pull away, recede inside herself to a place even I might not be able to reach her.

"Take the rest of the day off, Charlotte. Your work is suffering." I brushed past her.

CHAPTER
29

Charlotte

He had left me in the worst place I could be.

Alone with my thoughts.

Staring at the ceiling, I stood just inside the doorway.

I wouldn't admit it to anyone that I was giving myself a moment, waiting for any sign that I was about to burst into flames of hellfire just for being here.

But, of course, nothing happened.

As Frank had said, *this isn't the movies.*

No matter how old I was, the magnitude of this building still awed me. As a child, I had only been to this heritage church in the city once. I remembered looking out the window as we drove home, watching the tall church disappear over the horizon, wanting to watch it until the spire was lost from view. The entire world outside seemed somehow less impressive after being inside the church, even the city didn't hold the same glamor as it had on the drive in.

Running my fingers over the intricate carving in the pillars, I moved toward the front of the large space, passing through the dappled sunlight cast through the stained-glass windows that towered above me. The disturbed dust moved through the sunlight and made me feel as though I was walking through the light itself, the air filled with the Holy Spirit.

I reached the altar at the center of the sanctuary, unburned, and for a moment forgot myself, staring at the cross before kneeling and bowing my head.

Lord.

I stopped. What exactly was I here for? To ask for forgiveness?

There was no point in doing that unless I didn't intend to see Frank again and planned on somehow making up for the fact I had begun a bonding process with a damn demon.

Hey, God, I fucked a demon. I'm sure you understand I want to do it again.

Was I here to have the choice made for me? I was fairly certain God didn't work that way, giving you straight-out answers to yes or no questions. I had never tried asking so directly, but to not figure this out for myself would somehow feel like a failure.

So, I wouldn't ask then.

If I wasn't here to ask, it brought me back to the first question, *why was I here?*

I started to tremble in the church, despite the sunlight on my back, feeling as though God was watching my every move, waiting for me to make the right one. The warmth on my shoulders did nothing to abate the cool of my knees on the hard floor.

Lord, please...

I sighed against my hands, cupped at the bridge of my nose with my head bowed. Opening my eyes, I stared at the worn carpet beneath my knees from thousands of other parishioners kneeling in this sacred place, asking for forgiveness or guidance or simply to connect. Straining my hearing, I couldn't find the sounds of anyone else moving around the church. There were no services today, and it seemed I had at least this space to myself.

So, what was I to do with this time?

I think I love him.

The thought struck me like a bolt of lightning, unaware that it was creeping up from my subconscious until it presented itself to me at the same time I had revealed it to God.

I waited, waited for retribution for what I had done, what I was feeling. But none came. There was no answer, no voice telling me I was doing something wrong. Surely, I was, though? He was a *demon*, a literal demon.

How could I even begin to process that?

Could he still be a good man in need of healing and a partner?

Could I be that person to him?

I didn't question this when I was with him, so was there an answer in that? With him, I felt safe, reassured, more myself than I had in years, more myself than I did when I was alone. I was free, he had freed me from the restraints that I had put on myself and had been put on me. He had rescued me from the nightmares of my childhood, nightmare that had ceased since the beginning of the bond. He was a protector, a lover. No amount of soul searching, of finding that balance between being out of my comfort zone and finding my place, had led me to feel as complete as I did when I was with him.

But there was baggage in a relationship, and there was *this*...

I wasn't sure what I was expecting.

Divine intervention, perhaps?

Answers to all my questions to come to me clearly and without judgment.

While there was no judgment here, there was inside me. I was judging myself and everything I had done in my life that had led me to this moment.

The emptiness of the church began to bother me, prickling at my skin with the silence. I could feel the presence of God here, and it didn't feel hateful or vengeful. I wasn't afraid, not of the church, not of God. The only thing I was really afraid of was the unknown, but it all came down to one question.

Did I trust Frank with my life?

I stood, straightening my skirt and casting another look at the cross, memorizing the lines of it, because who knew if I'd want to return once this was all said and done. I tried to ignore the echoes of my heels, following me like another presence as I left. I slowed as I approached the doors, a feeling of finality I couldn't explain flooding my body. I knew the answer to the question, so why didn't it make this any easier?

Did I trust Frank with my life?

Yes.

Frank

I'd tried doing it her way.

I tried to allow Charlotte the time I thought she'd benefit from to think, to get it all wrapped up in her head in a neat little fucking package.

But it had been four days, and she hadn't been into work since I had dismissed her at the beginning of the week, calling in sick each day direct to Human Resources rather than letting me know.

It's not like she didn't have my number.

When HR had asked me if I wanted a sick certificate from her, I was tempted to say yes. I wanted to force her into a situation that would make her uncomfortable and make her talk to a doctor about *why* she didn't feel up to coming to work and would rather sit at home and dwell on everything.

Assuming that's what she was doing.

I didn't know for sure as I had tried calling a handful of times, and she had never answered.

This couldn't be easy for her, but I was still angry, pacing my office as the hours of the day ticked on. My mind conjured images of her packing up the boxes she had only recently unpacked, moving out of the city, away from me, without telling me first. This just served to increase my anger, and while I knew I was being irrational, reacting to a situation that may not exist, I couldn't help it.

I couldn't help myself when it came to her.

Perhaps she was bringing out the humanity in me, and *dammit*, that did nothing to quench the rage rising in my chest.

I *was* going to wait until the weekend to go see her, but fuck it, I couldn't wait any longer.

"Meetings the rest of the day. Don't call me," I barked at the receptionist as I strode past.

She watched me cross the foyer with her mouth open in shock. I'd never particularly liked her, but I had never been outright rude to her before either. I remembered her interview, the way she sashayed into the office expecting the world on a platter because she knew how to pout and balance on pinpoint heels. She was hired partially for her qualifications and partially because I knew I'd never have any interest in trying to fuck her.

I drove fuming, slamming my foot on the brake just in time when I saw a cop approaching. The last thing I needed right now was to be pulled over for speeding. I didn't have the car booked in until next week to replace the lining of my trunk to get rid of the claw marks.

Mike would pay me back for that damage, I swear.

I was on edge, my susceptibility to an emotional reaction due to the actions of a human was bothering me. Reminding myself that she wasn't just any human, I gritted my teeth. It was Charlotte, and she was *my* human. Glancing at the police car in my rearview mirror as it pulled out of sight, I scowled at being forced to slow down.

Rules, petty rules.

What I didn't need was to be reminded by Mike about breaking Earth rules.

Although, I smirked, Mike would never again have the higher ground when it came to reminding me to keep a low profile. At least *I* had never slaughtered a house full of drug dealers and gang members.

That night had returned to my thoughts often, about Charlotte's question of whether God cared if demons were on Earth. Of course, He cared, and I had told her as long as we weren't committing mass murder, God would leave us be. But here we were still after Mike's frenzy, and there had been no repercussions. While I imagined those men who were destined to spend eternity in hell for their sins, even I hoped God didn't work in such ways as to have them cross paths with a demon about to snap to find their retribution. Perhaps Mike finding them was God's will. It was a dark thought. Apart from feeling wrong and grating against my insides, it made me feel like a pawn.

This just angered me further.

I narrowly avoided hitting a pedestrian as I swung into the parking spot.

When I banged on Charlotte's door, she didn't answer.

Undeterred, I tried again, shouting through the closed door, "Charlotte, it's me, I just want to talk." I failed to keep the edge from my voice, and the part of me that was concerned if I was scaring her was being firmly pushed back into place by the irritation that grew within me.

Whatever small sounds I could hear from inside the apartment silenced, so I tilted my head placing my ear closer to the door, but still hearing nothing.

I was out of patience.

"I swear to God, Charlotte, I'll knock this door off its fucking hinges!"

I expected her to be angry, to fight fire with fire, and answer my threat with the same rage that boiled in me. But the door opened slowly, and she simply stood there in the gap, one hand still poised on the handle and the other on the doorframe. My eyes raked her body—she was wearing a loose t-shirt and baggy shorts, no makeup, and her long hair in a plait that fell down her back. She didn't look like she had been sleeping well or been outside at all, paler than usual with dark circles under her eyes. She had recently showered, though. I could smell the subtle floral perfume from the soap on her skin.

Damn, she was still beautiful.

CHAPTER
30

Frank

"Can I come in?" I growled.

Charlotte shrugged, then nodded, dropping her arm from the door frame and waiting for me to pass before closing the door behind me. She walked straight past me, ignoring the way my shoulders and arms tensed when she got close, and returned to the sink to finish washing the dishes.

Taking in the apartment, I released a breath. She had been unpacking, not packing up. I felt a fresh wave of relief wash over me.

The fact I felt relief flickered the irritation inside me again.

This whole *caring* about someone thing was bullshit.

Sitting on a stool at the kitchen island, I watched her wash the dishes. She didn't say anything or meet my eyes at all, but she was more than aware of my proximity. Her cheeks flushed with color where before there was none, her breathing only slightly uneven, but it was enough for me to pick up on. I simply watched her, displaying patience I didn't know I had.

Although even I couldn't stop the drumming of my fingers on the counter.

The seconds passed, turning into minutes.

I watched her hands as she was running water over a plate that was clearly already clean. When I looked at her face again, her eyes were brimming with tears. Reaching over, I turned the faucet off as she dropped the dish into the sink with a hollow clunk. Standing, I walked around the island and leaned my hip against it as I reached her. Taking her shoulders, I turned her to face me, but she kept her gaze firmly on her feet.

"Charlotte…"

"This is *crazy*, Frank!" The words exploded out of her at the same moment she looked at me. As soon as I had broken the silence, it all came tumbling out. She stuttered, she picked items up and put them back down, she went to turn away and would turn back. "I mean, I don't even know if I can get my head around what's going on. I was *so sure* of everything and thought I finally had my life in order. Maybe one day I'd find someone to settle down with and get married, and then *you* come along and turn my world upside-down. Demons, Frank. *Demons!* Seriously? How is this even a thing I'm having to think about right now? How am I even supposed to begin sorting through this?"

I watched her eyes. All these thoughts had been bundled up inside her for days or longer. She hadn't spoken to anyone, how could she? But she could've come to me, talked to me, asked me questions. By hiding away, all she did was allow these thoughts to run rampant in her mind, with no escape and no one to offer consolation or help. She had been arguing with herself and gotten nowhere. I let her talk until she took a long deep breath, and after asking conflicting questions one after the other, she finally looked at me.

"I want you," she said, her voice a quiet reflection of the passion from a moment ago. "I want you in my life so much. I feel lost and alone when you're not around. That kind of commitment has never scared me, but this is so much more complicated."

"Is it?"

"Of *course,* it is."

I sighed. "I really wish you had come and talked to me. You've worked yourself into a frenzy."

"You sent me home."

"Not *indefinitely.*"

"I needed some time to think."

"And how has that worked out for you?"

She glared at me. "Don't you be a smartass with

me. This is a big thing."

I held my arms open, taking a step back from her and waiting for her to look me in the eyes again before I spoke, "It's me, Charlotte, it is just me. You know what I am, but you also know *who* I am." I dropped my arms. "I could've helped you figure this out. I still can." When she opened her mouth to speak, I held up my hand, smirking at the way she pouted in response. "I'm still not pressuring you, but if you want me, I'm here."

"I want you," she mumbled.

I took a step closer. "Sorry, I didn't quite catch that?"

She hesitated, firmly ignoring the smirk that passed across my face before lifting her hand, then dropping it again after brushing over my shirt. "I've thought about nothing but this for days, over and over in my head, and I always come back to the same answer." When she looked at me, her eyes were clear. "I want you, and I want you and me together. Whatever that entails."

Pausing, I wanted to hold on to my anger, to keep it inside for what she put me through by cutting me off. I wanted to throw that back at her, tell her how much it hurt, and all because of how much I care about her. I wanted her to know that the fact I hurt at all, that I was experiencing *any* feelings, was also painful for me to deal with.

But damn.

She was so close, and hearing her saying she wanted me, to be *with* me, flushed all the anger from my body. I bent slightly, kissing her as she tilted her face up to mine. Softly moving my lips against hers, tracing lines around her neck with my fingertips before wrapping my hand around her throat but not squeezing, making her moan as I moved my tongue into her mouth.

"Do you want to finish the bond?" I questioned against her lips.

She nodded, pulling at her t-shirt. "Do we need to…"

I chuckled and stilled her hands. "No, we don't need to be having sex. Maybe it's better if we don't. I want you to have a clear head, and we both know what I do to you."

She started to laugh, glared at me, then she flushed. The series of reactions made me chuckle. I knew I could find places in her, under her skin and into her very being, places no one else had touched but me.

"I'm scared," she whispered.

"Of me?"

"Of the unknown."

I kissed the top of her head and pulled her into a hug as she pressed her cheek against my chest. "There's nothing to be afraid of. You're with me."

And I meant it.

Nothing will hurt you, Charlotte, not ever. Not now

that you have me, and I have you.

Tilting her head up to my face, for the first time, she saw pain in my eyes. I had been hiding it, but the way her expression softened, I knew I was hiding no more. I'd told her I would be okay if she chose not to be with me, but that was a lie.

My intentions had been only to protect her. So adamant in my resolve to have her come to me, I'd pretended to be indifferent about her decision because I didn't want her to be scared or obligated. If this was real, then she had to come to me on her own.

"I have told no one, opened up to no one, no one but you. I'm not sure what I would've done if you rejected me."

"What will I become, really?"

"You'll be human but with demon blood. It will extend your lifespan, increase your senses and your reactions. But you'll still be human, just bonded to me, and I to you."

She stared at me for a beat before her eyes widened. "Will I grow a tail?" she cried.

The seriousness of the situation was lost for a moment, and I laughed. "A tail?"

"In my nightmares... sometimes there was a tail."

The guilt for laughing at her fear crept up the back of my neck. "We don't have tails, Charlotte. Part of the tricks of an attack is to induce fear through hallucinations, usually driven from your fears from movies or stories." I considered her. "Or your own perceived images of demons and devils."

She was twisting her hands together but nodded while I tried to keep myself steady, reminding myself that all of these questions were natural, that she really did want me, and she wasn't going to leave me.

I half expected her to ask what *The* Devil actually looked like.

She didn't.

Probably for the best.

"I still don't quite understand what the bonding means."

I thought, trying to think about the best way to describe it. "We will be connected on a base level. You may feel discomfort if we are too far apart. You'll feel disgusted by other men too close and enraged when women are too close to me."

She laughed, then studied my face. "You're serious?"

"It's the power of the bond." I shrugged.

She took my hands and nodded. "I'm ready."

I gave her a final appraising glance, flitting my eyes between hers. There was still that seed of doubt within me that she'd change her mind, which would be worse now that I had allowed myself to feel hope and expressed to her my fears of losing her. But Charlotte stared at me with such intensity, when I saw the yellow phase across her eyes, I knew she was telling the truth.

She was ready, and this is what she wanted.

In a way, we were already connected. It was strong enough that she was willing to throw her remaining questions to the side and figure them out as she goes, as long as it meant we were together.

CHAPTER
31

Charlotte

He took my hand and led me to the couch, pulling me down gently next to him before removing his shirt. I watched him move, such formality to his motions, one button at a time before draping it over the back of the couch, as though this were the end of the workday and not the beginning of something life-changing. When he saw me watching his hands, he grinned, that smile that melted me from the inside out, and any doubt I had left was washed away.

There wasn't much doubt left anyway.

Spend the rest of my life with this man? Abso-fucking-lutely.

When he was naked from the waist up, I stared at his chest until he cleared his throat and raised my eyes to his smug face. "Don't worry, you can touch me soon enough."

"I wasn't…" I protested, my voice trailing off at the knowing look in his eye. I swallowed. "Do you… uh, want a knife or something?"

"No." He looked at his hands. "The wound needs to be inflicted with my hands…" he raised his eyes to mine and added, "… or yours."

"I can't… I don't think… I mean—"

"It's okay."

Taking a deep breath, I held it as he dragged a nail across his chest, reopening the wound from our previous session. The skin had healed, but the memory of the night was imprinted in my mind, and I recognized the place the cut had been, remembered the taste of his skin and blood. I found myself biting my lower lip in anticipation. Frank lifted one arm over the back of the couch and watched me, waiting for me to make the move.

Although I did move slower than I had planned, I didn't hesitate, two raging instincts fighting against each other—one to rush forward and take him, another to savor the moment. His arms strained with the effort of staying still as I slid across the couch until I was nestled next to him. I wished I had put more effort into my appearance, but how was I to know today would be the most important day? I didn't like being caught out without makeup or in my crappiest clothes even at the shops. But Frank didn't seem to mind, and he was watching my lips with a hungry look in his eyes as I lowered my mouth to his chest.

When he felt my breath hot against his skin, Frank tensed up. "Are you sure you want this?" he asked again. He grabbed my shoulders to make me look at him, and with a betraying twitch of his arms, I was sure he was about to yank me toward him.

As my lips poised above the blood on his skin, I looked up at him through my lashes. "Yes," I answered. "Do you?"

He let my shoulders go, returning his arm over the back of the couch, and was mid-nod when I pressed my lips to his skin. Lapping at the wound tentatively with my tongue, he groaned, gripping the back of the couch.

When I heard the fabric protest and rip, I didn't care.

I didn't think I needed to take much—the last time I had taken barely any at all. But I moaned against his skin, taking in more of him as my fingers splayed across his abdomen, holding him still when he started to squirm under my touch. The blood changed in my mouth, the sickly metallic tang melding with me, and the taste became sweet.

Insatiable.

The squirming sensation in my stomach grew and then eased as my body put up a fight against the intrusion of the demon blood for as long as it could against the stronger force. I could feel it working through my veins, spreading under my skin and into every part of me.

I'd never get enough of him.

Frank

"Charlotte, please…" I moaned as she sucked at the wound. "Stop. You don't need to…"

I moaned again as she pressed her hand to my stomach, pushing me down and taking more blood. She didn't stop, and I looked down at her mouth around my pectoral and her pupils expanding, flooding her eyes with black before the yellow took over. She was moaning and writhing against me.

Still, she didn't stop.

I grabbed her hair and pulled, and she resisted, sucking on the cut. But she couldn't fight against my strength for long, and she released the suction on my skin with a pop. I clasped my other hand over the open wound as it began to bleed freely, watching the now thin slits of her pupils dart between my mouth and chest.

Blood could be addictive. I knew that better than most. Mike saved me from my addiction and brought me to live on Earth with him, like the big brother I never had.

Or did, I had hundreds, but kinship was not strong within demons. They preferred the company of their bonded partner over their birth family.

Charlotte licked her lips—the taste of my blood would still be rich in her mouth. Her lips were full and swollen from her attack on me, and still she tugged against my grip on her hair, desperate to take more. When our eyes met, I allowed mine to slide into their natural yellow too, and when I smirked, she smiled back. Nothing else in the world mattered. The entire apartment could've been an empty void with only her and I and this couch floating through eternity. There were a thousand invisible threads holding us together, and every inch she was apart from me was agony.

I had never bonded before, nor knew of many who had bonded with humans, but as I watched her chest rise and fall with the increase in her breathing, I could hear her heart pounding inside her chest. Almost instinctively, I wrapped my hand around the back of her neck, caressing the skin.

No matter how desperately I wanted to take her now, I needed to teach her.

"Control yourself, Charlotte," I whispered, my voice a soothing rumble working from my throat into her soul. "Feel it, take it in, but control it. Don't let it control you." I watched as she closed her eyes, forcing her breathing to steady.

Charlotte, always so in control, a fast learner, a passionate being.

The perfect mate.

"Come back to me. Open your eyes." I crooned, and when she looked back at me, her eyes were human, meeting the dark brown of mine. "How do you feel?"

She didn't answer but grabbed my shoulders and pulled herself forward, her chest hitting mine, and my arms winding around her as she kissed me. She moved across, kissing the side of my mouth and then my cheek, kissing her way down my neck and over my shoulder, playfully biting at my skin. I groaned, my fingers gripping her shoulders in warning as I pushed her away when she got too close to the wound again. She frowned at me as I smiled, taking in her delightfully swollen lips and flushed cheeks.

In my mind, a repetition of the mantra *she's mine* over and over again.

She's mine.

"Stand up," I commanded. "Strip for me."

Charlotte

When I stood, Frank kicked the cardboard box that acted as my coffee table out of the way and sent it sliding across the floor. He unbuckled his pants and pulled them down over his legs, leaving him in only his boxers. I stood in front of him, taking in the muscular form of his perfect body, his thighs just begging to be clawed. He reached forward and slapped the curve of my ass, making me jump.

"Did you misunderstand or are you intentionally disobeying me?" he growled, sending a shiver down my spine. "Strip."

I pulled the t-shirt over my head, breaking eye contact with him only for the moment my vision obscured by the fabric. Tossing it to the side, I reached for the elastic waist of my shorts, reveling in the way his eyes flashed as I gradually pulled them over my hips and thighs, letting gravity take over and dropping them to the floor before stepping out of the tangle. I unhooked my bra, and when Frank noticed how my chest arched toward him when I twisted my arm behind my back, I enunciated the motion. By the time I had removed my panties, his cock was achingly hard against his boxers.

"Who owns you?" he asked.

"You do," I whispered, barely able to keep the breath to answer any louder.

I licked my lips as I watched him rubbing himself through his boxers, the outline of his cock was clearly visible, hard in his grip, and I bit my lip when he noticed me watching and kept rubbing.

He grinned.

Dangerous.

Promising.

"Prove it."

Once on my knees, I crawled toward him. He pulled his boxers off as I approached and spread his legs so I could kneel between his feet. Eyeing him, I waited for my next instruction.

Feeling my control slip, my eyes glazed over when his cock came free of its constraints. He pumped it in his hand a few times, enjoying my discomfort at not being able to act, testing my control, but also enjoying his dominance over me.

I was right where I wanted to be—naked and on my knees in front of him.

"Open your mouth."

Obeying immediately, Frank's smirk almost turned into a snarl, and he grabbed my plait, guiding my head down. Sliding his cock into my mouth all the way, he drew it back out just as slowly. He groaned as he repeated the motion, his grip on me loosening as I took control and continued the steady rhythm. He let me go for a short while, then took my hair again, grinning at the small gasp that escaped my lips as he pulled himself from my mouth.

"Stick your tongue out." Again, I obeyed, and again he slid his cock into my mouth, gliding it across my welcoming tongue and moaning loudly. "Oh, fuck, Charlotte, that feels so fucking good." I simply moaned in response, the sound reverberating across his sensitive skin. Bit by bit, he increased his speed, channeling all his control until he was thrusting into my mouth, lifting his hips from the couch toward me while pulling my head to him.

"Stand up."

He yanked on my hair, pulling his cock from my mouth, releasing a gasp as I stood on shaky legs. Running his hands up the back of my thighs and over my ass, he gripped the flesh beneath his fingers and hummed his approval. I didn't know where to look, taking in his arms—the way his muscles flexed as he held me—his chest, the delicious V-shape of his abdomen, as though it were an arrow pointing down to his waiting cock, hard and dripping with precum and my saliva.

"Come to me," Frank mumbled, his words almost lost in lust. Everything we had felt together previously was amplified now that we were bonded. I straddled him, and he never let go of my thighs as I lowered myself onto him, taking him inside me in one smooth motion. His pupils dilated as he studied the arch of my neck, licking the lines of my collarbone leading to my breasts which were pushed toward him as I arched into his touch. His cock stretched me open to accommodate him, and I ached for more.

When he was fully sheathed inside me, he started moving—small, unhurried thrusts, relishing in the squeeze of me around him. I matched his motion, moving in tandem with him, my hands on his shoulders and his on my waist, his fingers gripped and flexed as he twitched inside me.

I watched his face. Beyond the pleasure of the physical act, I could tell there was so much going on inside that head. Hoping it was all good things, I didn't want him experiencing any regrets or fear. All I wanted was to be there for him as much as he was for me.

Oh, Frank, tell me what's going on in that head of yours.

CHAPTER
32

Frank

She leaned her forehead against mine, closing her eyes, and I tried to focus only on the feel of her around me. I wanted to tell her no and move her back so I could watch her. I wanted to instruct her, to control her. But she was so close, closer than I could remember ever being to anyone. Beyond the physical connection of being inside her and around her, she was *with* me.

She was with me emotionally, mentally, and spiritually.

For obvious reasons, I'd never much focused on the spiritual side, but my connection with her couldn't be explained any other way. I kept my eyes open, wanting to watch her. The blurry outline of her face was so close to mine, I couldn't focus on any one feature. When she opened her eyes, I drank in the hazel coloring, and she watched me.

"Frank," she whispered, reaching up and cupping my cheek in her palm.

I snatched her wrist with an involuntary snarl. "Don't." My voice broke, and when she focused on my face, I know she saw the pain and the battle. I didn't want her to see it, but there was no hiding from her anymore. My face crumpled as I struggled with the feelings I was experiencing.

"Don't," I repeated, barely a whisper.

"Why?" she murmured.

My grip on her wrist loosened. "I can't…" How could I explain it to her? I had never bonded before, so how was I to know it would feel like this? How was I to explain I didn't know what to do with these feelings?

"Yes, you can." She stroked my cheek with her thumb. "I love you."

My eyes darted between hers, and she smiled sadly while she waited. She knew the reply. Of course, she did. I'd already taken the ultimate step for my kind. I know that she knew. But she wanted to hear me say it, she was still human, and she needed to hear the words.

She wanted me to say them.

Why was this so hard?

"I love you too."

When she pressed her lips to mine, I ran my hand through her hair, twisting around her plait again. I turned the kiss dirty, licking the inside of her mouth and sucking on her tongue. It was too much, the vulnerability, feeling so open and exposed. She could read everything about me now through our connection.

It was too much.

Thrusting up into her harder, I swallowed her moans as I fucked her. I loved the gasps she made when I pulled away from her mouth and she hungrily took in the air before taking back the kiss with equal fervor.

"I want to take you." I panted, needing to reclaim her, to take back some of the control I had lost. Yanking on her hair, I forced her back to arch before running my tongue up her neck toward her chin and nipping at her bottom lip.

"So, take me."

Lifting her off my lap, she sighed as she was left feeling empty. Standing, I walked around the couch, bending her over the side and moving behind her. Poising my cock by her pussy, I rubbed the head between the wet folds, my smile twisted every time she jumped when I ran it over her clit. My hips began small thrusts forward, stretching her open with the head before leaving her empty again. She was begging me to put it inside, wanting the stretch, her legs pressed close together only making her entrance tighter.

I groaned as I pushed the head in and left it still, shuddering as she clamped around me, desperate to keep me inside.

"Tell me to stop if I hurt you," I said, warning edging on my voice. I didn't want her to feel pain, not too much, but I needed to release, and to claim. My inner demon was pleading to take control.

When she didn't reply, I grabbed her plait again, pulling her harshly until her face was angled to the ceiling.

"Tell me to stop if I hurt you." I snarled, the muscles in my arm swirling as the black exploded on my skin for a brief moment.

She replied only with a hum and a small moan, focusing on the feel of me inside her. She was dripping wet around me, and I could barely think of anything else but the sensation of her.

When I yanked her head back again, she cried out, and I growled, "You'll tell me if I hurt you!"

"Okay!" she cried, and as I let her hair go, she dropped her head onto the couch cushion, bracing herself when she felt my fingers on her hips.

The grip promised pain but also pleasure.

I pushed in before drawing almost all the way out again, then slammed into her. She moaned, and I waited a second for her to protest. When she didn't, I kept going at that pace—brutal, hard, and fast. Thrusting that would've pushed her forward were it not for my steel-like grip on her hips. I focused on her voice, and the moans and profanities dropping from her mouth were a turn-on in themselves.

She was letting go the way I wanted her to.

I was letting go too.

She gasped when I pulled out and dropped to my knees, pushing my face between her thighs and flicking my tongue over her clit. Her fingers clawed and gripped the couch as I buried my face into her, taking her clit between my lips and sucking.

"Frank, I'm going to..." She gasped, scrambling to hold herself together as she felt the orgasm build. I only went harder, expertly licking and sucking, gripping her thighs hard enough to bruise. When she came, I kept going, moaning against the folds of her skin as she shook and struggled under my touch. Pushing through the waves of her orgasm, I kept going until she was a panting mess bent over the arm of the couch. So, when I stood and slammed my cock into her again, her back arched as I stretched her open, tightened after her climax.

Resuming the relentless pace, I pounded into her with unbridled strength and gripped her legs, almost lifting her off the couch and thrusting into her. Spasming, I missed a beat as my orgasm approached, and she keened for the feel of me exploding inside of her, filling her with my seed. When I came, the sound that escaped me was a roar of possession, a cross between human and demon laying claim to the woman who squirmed under my touch.

The animalistic growls continued as I gently leaned over her, rocking my hips, my cock still hard inside her. Charlotte had collapsed, limp from both the explosion of her orgasm and the brutal pace I had taken her with.

She better be ready again soon.

Watching her, it occurred to me this was beyond what I had anticipated. The reality of bonding with a human meant more than her taking on my traits, but me taking on some of hers.

I *cared* for her beyond the possessiveness I had felt since day one. I truly cared.

It seemed as much as I brought out the demon in her, she brought out the human in me.

Charlotte

He had literally ruined me for all other men.

I grinned into the cushion. Even if we hadn't bonded, no one else could fuck me like that.

Fuck.

He withdrew slowly, and I clenched around him, making him chuckle and release a heavy breath as my muscles gripped against the sensitive head of his cock. Collapsing on the couch next to me, I crawled over the couch's arm and moved against him, sighing into his form as he wrapped an arm around my shoulders. I took him in, running my fingertips up his cock, still standing at attention. He jumped at my touch, smiling with his eyes closed as his head tilted back against the couch.

"Do you want to go again, pet?" he whispered.

I simply hummed, tracing the lines of his cock with my fingertips. "Looks like you're still ready for me."

His fingers gripped my shoulder. "I'll always be ready for you."

I climbed onto his lap and lowered myself on top of him again, taking him inside me and moaning with him at the stretch. That delicious stretch that I'll never get enough of, and now, would never have to be without.

I moved with him, slowly.

There was no rush. The desire stirred inside me, fueling me. But I kept it under control, taking my time, noticing the smirk that spread across his lips.

Smug bastard.

He straightened his back, running his hands up my spine and over my shoulders before pulling me down to him, groaning with me. I was learning control. It would take time, but I was learning. When I leaned my forehead against his, he stilled and let me move.

Out of nowhere, he whispered. "Stay with me."

I opened my eyes, watching his face so close to

mine, but his eyes were still closed.

"I'm with you," I answered, my voice a gentle breeze against his skin.

He looked troubled, and a hint of a frown adorned his face as he tightened his arms around my waist, pulling me closer into him—chest to chest—connected in every way. I could feel his breath against my lips as he continued to move within me, missing a beat every now and then. I could feel the demon blood stirring within me, and if I focused on him so close to me, I could sense the blood moving within his veins too.

I realized I wanted to taste it, to bite him, to drink his life.

Maybe I didn't yet have the control I thought I did.

"Frank," I whispered, he hummed. "I don't know how to do this."

"Fuck? You'll learn."

I pulled a face. "Very funny. No, I mean, how to be a demon."

He opened his eyes to meet mine, yellow on yellow. I knew he could feel my desperation for control, he knew me well enough by now. His lips curved into a snarl, and he growled his approval.

I was fighting for control only he could teach me.

"I'll show you," he said.

EPILOGUE

Charlotte

My eyes traveled to Mike as I passed him in the hall. Throwing him a casual glance even as my skin prickled at his proximity, I neither challenged nor accepted him being this close to me. Of course, I harbored no ill feelings toward Mike, but the bond was complete, and he was an opposing demon within our bonded territory.

I could almost see his skin crawling beneath his shirt as he resisted to urge to plaster himself against the opposite wall until I passed. Our closeness to each other in these moments was not only a discomfort for me.

He nodded at me, and I smiled sweetly, but neither of us broke stride, not wanting to prolong the unpleasant sensation.

As we cleared each other's space, I breathed out

a heavy sigh. In the past three months, I had worked hard at gaining control of myself, including my inner demon. Frank's blood had melded to mine as though it belonged, and I felt it did belong.

Once I had relinquished control, I was able to claw it back, stronger than before.

I was on my way to my desk outside Frank's office, having just had a second interview with another architecture firm. Of course, Frank was aware of the interview, but that didn't mean he had to be happy about it. I could practically feel the rumble of his growl against the skin on my neck as I told him what I wanted to do. I smirked, he may have agreed, but compromise was still something he was working on. His instinct ran thick within him.

The interview had given me a good feeling, and having progressed to the second stage was a good sign. While I wouldn't be designing straight away, if I succeeded, I would be partnered with an architect who would train me over the next twelve months before I'd be allowed to attempt my first solo project.

The other architect was a woman. I had already checked.

I snickered to myself. Frank would fry a circuit if I had to work in close quarters with another man. I was testing his limits even by applying for another job, but he had wanted a mate and a partner, not a slave, and with that came acceptance that I had my own path to follow.

But, of course, I'd always be coming home to him, undoing my buttons and skirt zipper on my way to the front door. I knew he'd be on me the moment I crossed the threshold, and constantly having to replace my torn clothes was getting costly.

As I rounded the corner to my desk, my skin started to prickle again. This time a pleasant sensation, a warmth rising through my body starting at my extremities and working its way to my chest, increasing with every step I took closer to Frank.

As he came into my line of vision, I stopped. He was standing in front of his desk, feet firmly planted shoulder-width apart, and his arms crossed over his impressive chest. The sight of him was breathtaking, even if he did have a deep frown furrowing his brow.

But something was off.

My brow knitted together as I moved to him, slower than before. I stopped only a foot away from him. He didn't move, simply watched me slink toward him as I sniffed the air between us.

"Who is *that*?" I asked. My tone was more aggressive than I had intended, but Frank was unfazed, his lips curling into a smirk that was almost a snarl.

"I could ask you the same thing?" His voice was a

deep purr that ran across his tongue and touched me without him needing to move. My lip curled, and I could smell the scent of another woman on him and his hands.

He grinned as he watched my eyes. "A handshake. I was interviewing your potential replacement." When my nose twitched and my frown deepened, the smell of another woman assaulting my senses, Frank's smile grew wider. "Annoying, isn't it?"

"I also had an interview." I pushed the words through gritted teeth as Frank approached me, closing the space between us and standing chest to chest with me. His stupid grin was starting to grate against me—he was enjoying this. It was another lesson I had to learn about what it meant to be bonded with a demon—this pain.

"Hurts, doesn't it?" he crooned. His skin was prickling with the scent of another man having been around me. I knew it, but he was clearly enjoying my reaction to him. He wanted to push me, to make me jealous, to test my control and see what would happen.

I hated to admit it was totally working.

The man knew how to push my buttons.

He continued, "You can smell her beyond her lingering perfume. You know she was close to me. You can almost see her sweet little face in your mind, can't you? She used to be a dancer, you know?

She offered to dance for me."

"No, she didn't." It wasn't a question, but the sneer was growing on Frank's already smug face.

"No, she didn't. But it's fun to mess with you."

Frank chuckled quietly when a low growl worked its way up my throat, and he leaned in close to me, his lips brushing against my neck before his breath was at my ear. Although he didn't move his hands, I relished in the feel of my chest rising and falling against his. He threw a glance over my shoulder toward the hallway.

"What are you going to do about it?" he teased.

With the way he pouted slightly, he was obviously expecting me to kiss him, to lay my claim on him that way. So, when my hand shot up and gripped at his collar and tie, bunching it up in my fist and drawing his face to mine, he grinned. I growled again before leaning closer to him, his laugh breaking off into a moan when I closed my teeth and lips around his neck by his collar and bit into his skin. When I felt the skin break, he moved with lightning-fast reactions and grabbed my wrists, forcing my hands to my sides and glaring at me as I smirked, licking his blood from my teeth.

"Not the face," I said in a sing-song voice, enjoying his reaction at my tease. He was great at dishing it out but not so good at taking it.

He snarled.

My smile faltered.

Spinning me around on the spot, he pinned my arms to my chest with one of his wrapped around my torso. Half-leading and half-dragging me across his office, he swiped an arm angrily across his desk, clearing it of the papers at this moment he didn't care for. I moaned as he bent me over his desk and pressed himself against me. I could feel the outline of his cock through his pants as it hardened.

He leaned over me, grinding his hips against me as his hands explored my body. "Ready, pet?"

"Always," I whispered.

THE END

Next in the Unearthly Sins Series
The Angel in Her

ACKNOWLEDGMENTS

Thank you to my beta readers for your feedback and encouragement.

As always to my partner for his on-going support.

To my editors for their expertise and assistance.

To everyone who accepts the dark recesses of my mind that produce these stories and embraces it with me.

Connect WITH ME ONLINE

ANGELS AND FIRE BOOKS
Find our exciting stories at:
www.angelsandfirebooks.com.au

READER GROUP

Want access to fun, prizes and sneak peeks?
Join my Facebook Reader Group.
https://www.facebook.com/groups/588038442170571

Stefanie Dawn

NEWSLETTER

Sign up for my Newsletter.
https://www.subscribepage.com/angelsandfirebooks

GOODREADS

Add my books to your TBR list
on my Goodreads profile.
https://www.goodreads.com/author/
show/21761217.Stefanie_Dawn

AMAZON

https://www.amazon.com/author/stefaniedawn

WEBSITE

http://www.angelsandfirebooks.com.au/

INSTAGRAM

https://www.instagram.com/angelsandfirebooks

EMAIL

info@angelsandfirebooks.com.au

FACEBOOK

https://www.facebook.com/stefaniedawnwriter

About THE AUTHOR

Stefanie Dawn has been a writer and creative soul all her life **and** strives to give her readers stories that they can escape into as they become absorbed in the worlds created.

When she isn't writing, Stefanie might be painting, reading, or watching movies. She loves the process of producing films as another form of storytelling. There is also a good chance she will be baking some delicious treats—pretending she won't later regret consuming them—or simply enjoying a cocktail with friends.

Stefanie Dawn lives in South Australia with her ever-supportive partner and a lovable gang of rescue cats.

Stefanie Dawn

You can stay up to date with
Stefanie and her books at:
www.angelsandfirebooks.com.au

9 781763 870413